Frank

A Play in Two Acts

Dramatized by
Tim Kelly

From the classic by
Mary Shelley

A SAMUEL FRENCH ACTING EDITION

SAMUEL FRENCH
FOUNDED 1830
New York Hollywood London Toronto
SAMUELFRENCH.COM

Frankenstein

STORY OF THE PLAY

Victor Frankenstein, a brilliant young scientist, returns to his chateau on the shores of Lake Geneva to escape some terrible pursuer. No one can shake free the dark secret that terrifies him. Not his mother, nor his fiancee Elizabeth, nor his best friend, Henry Clerval. Even the pleading of a gypsy girl accused of murdering Victor's younger brother falls on deaf ears, for Victor has brought into being a "Creature" made from bits and pieces of the dead! The Creature tracks Victor to his sanctuary to demand a bride to share its loneliness—one as wretched as the Creature itself. Against his better judgment, Victor agrees and soon the household is invaded by murder, despair and terror! The play opens on the wedding night of Victor and Elizabeth, the very time the Creature has sworn to kill the scientist for destroying its intended mate, and ends, weeks later, in a horrific climax of dramatic suspense! In between there is enough macabre humor to relieve the mounting tension. Perhaps the truest adaptation of Mary Shelley's classic yet. Simple to stage and a guaranteed audience pleaser. Suitable for all groups.

3

Frankenstein

A Play in Two Acts
FOR FOUR MEN AND FOUR WOMEN

CHARACTERS
(*In Order of Appearance*)

ERNST ....*an Inspector-General of police*

SOPHIE. ....*a housekeeper*

VICTOR FRANKENSTEIN ....*a young scientist*

ELIZABETH ....*Victor's fiancee*

HENRY ....*Victor's friend, also a scientist*

FRAU FRANKENSTEIN ....*Victor's mother*

THE CREATURE ....*an artificially-created man*

JUSTINE ....*a gypsy girl*

SYNOPSIS

PLACE: A chateau on the shores of Lake Geneva, Switzerland.

TIME: Before the turn of the century.

ACT ONE

SCENE 1: The study of Victor Frankenstein. Evening.
SCENE 2: The same. Immediately following.
SCENE 3: The same. That evening.

ACT TWO

SCENE 1: The study. One week later.
SCENE 2: The same. Two days later.
SCENE 3: Same as Act One, Scene 1.

Frankenstein

ACT ONE

SCENE 1

SETTING: *The study of Victor Frankenstein. Down Right is a door that leads into an off-stage laboratory. Up Center is the main entrance into the room, with drapes that can be pulled across when required. There is a hallway beyond this entrance that leads off Up Right to an unseen door. Left and Right of the main entrance are rows and rows of books. French doors, also with drapes, are Stage Left with some outside garden foliage in view. A sofa is Stage Right and two fine chairs are Stage Left. Sofa and chairs are angled out to the audience for best sight lines possible. There is a desk and chair Down Left with a standing anatomy chart. This describes only the essentials. Naturally, additional stage dressing will greatly enhance the impact of the set; paintings, more books, small tables, occasional chairs, lamps, rugs, hunting trophies, vases, etc. The study is a darkish sort of enclave, shadowy but comfortable, reflecting masculine elegance and an aura of the academic.*

AT RISE: *Night. The room is softly lighted. Drapes Up Center and at the French doors are pulled aside. Moonlight illuminates the garden foliage. Stage remains empty for a moment and, then,* VOICES *behind the laboratory door.*

SOPHIE'S VOICE. (*Offstage.*) I don't understand. I don't understand any of it.

ERNST'S VOICE. It's not important what you do or do not understand. (ERNST, *a police commandant, in uniform, enters Right. He's an exacting man, well disciplined, a dedicated professional. He's followed by* SOPHIE, *the housekeeper. She's nervous and apprehensive.*)

SOPHIE. Police everywhere. In the garden. On the shores of the lake. (ERNST *has crossed Down Center, takes out his revolver, checks it.*)

ERNST. We've searched the house thoroughly.

SOPHIE. Yes, but why?

ERNST. You ask a great many questions, Sophie.

SOPHIE. I've earned that right.

ERNST. You're certain there's no other room or area of the chateau where anyone might hide? Or anything?

SOPHIE. What *thing?*

ERNST. One question at a time.

SOPHIE. (*Annoyed.*) I've been housekeeper for many years. I know of no other room or area of the chateau. (ERNST *checks the bullets.*)

ERNST. They say he's afraid of gunfire.

SOPHIE. Who? Herr Frankenstein?

ERNST. No, not him. (VOICES *from off Up Right.*)

ELIZABETH'S VOICE. (*Offstage.*) Victor, what are you doing?

VICTOR'S VOICE. (*Offstage.*) Only what tradition expects of me.

SOPHIE. They're back.

ERNST. Come on. Give them a few minutes of sanity.

SOPHIE. Sanity?

ERNST. Do as I tell you. (ERNST *moves to French doors, exits.*)

SOPHIE. (*Follows after him.*) No reception, no guests, police everywhere. Not my idea of a wedding night. (*We hear the laughter of* ELIZABETH *and shortly thereafter* VICTOR FRANKENSTEIN *appears Up Center with his bride in his arms.*)

ELIZABETH. (*Happily.*) Put me down, Victor. I'm out of breath. (VICTOR *is a young man, early twenties.*

Serious, tense, apprehensive. ELIZABETH *is younger by a year or so. She wears her bridal gown with style and clutches a bouquet of flowers.* VICTOR *puts her down and she moves toward the sofa.*)

VICTOR. Should I ring for Sophie?

ELIZABETH. What on earth for?

VICTOR. I thought you might want something to eat or drink. (*He glances nervously to the open French doors.*)

ELIZABETH. No, nothing. (*Then:*) Victor, now that we're married—won't you tell me what's been troubling you? (*He moves to the French doors, looks into the garden.*) You've been so distraught. When I speak, I'm not sure you hear what I say. When I look at you, I know your thoughts are elsewhere.

VICTOR. Forgive me, Elizabeth. (*Almost to himself.*) I have so much to be forgiven for.

ELIZABETH. (*Concerned.*) Victor? (*He turns.*) You . . . you don't regret marrying me? (*He crosses to her, takes her hand, kisses it.*)

VICTOR. I am afraid.

ELIZABETH. Afraid of what? (*Strong.*) Victor, you must tell me. You've lived these past months with some terrible private dread. I want to bring you happiness. (*Proud.*) I am Frau Frankenstein, the wife of a brilliant young scientist. Whatever troubles you, has to trouble me. I beg you, Victor. Take me into your confidence. (VICTOR *turns once again to the French doors.*) What's out there that frightens you?

VICTOR. (*Points.*) Tonight . . . this very night . . . the man who will kill me will come through those doors. (*ELIZABETH can barely speak, reacts.*)

ELIZABETH. What are you saying? (*She sits on the sofa, stunned.*)

VICTOR. I know it sounds incredible. Monstrous. All the same, it's true.

ELIZABETH. Who would want to kill you? Why? (*He sits beside her.*)

VICTOR. I ask only that you remember your love for me when you hear my words.

ELIZABETH. (*Wary.*) Go on . . .

VICTOR. Do you remember when I returned from the university at Ingolstadt?

ELIZABETH. Of course. You were in such poor health. We were all so worried for you.

VICTOR. I didn't want to return. . . . I wanted to find some icy glacier and build a funeral pyre . . . if not for myself, then for my deeds. . . . (*The stage lighting DIMS DOWN as* VICTOR *recollects the events of the past.* ELIZABETH *gets up and walks stately to the Up Center exit. Even in the dark her wedding gown will be semi-visible, so the actress should make her exit appear as part of the remembrance.* VICTOR's *words continue in the near-blackness.*) I hadn't slept in days . . . my brain was on fire. . . . I was consumed with guilt and fear . . . and that private dread you speak of. . . . (*The stage now is in total blackness.* ELIZABETH *is out. From off Left we hear the* VOICE *of* HENRY CLERVAL.)

HENRY'S VOICE. (*Offstage.*) Victor? Victor, are you in there . . . ?(*LIGHTS DIM UP for daylight.* VICTOR *is still sitting on the sofa.*) Victor? (VICTOR *stands as* HENRY *comes in via the open French doors carrying a book.*) Ah, there you are.

VICTOR. How are you, Henry?

HENRY. (*Moves* CENTER.) Question is, how are you?

VICTOR. Constant. My temper is almost violent. My mood varies between deep depression and melancholia.

HENRY. (*Attempts to jar him out of his somberness.*) Come, come, Victor, you're away from your gloomy university. What could be more pleasant than a holiday on the shores of Lake Geneva in one's own chateau?

VICTOR. Holiday? Call it retreat. Sanctuary. Anything but holiday. I appreciate your good spirits, Henry.

I know you're trying to cheer me up. It can't be much fun for anyone having me about like this.

HENRY. You've had a slight breakdown, that's all. Understandable, considering the way you drive yourself. For a young man, you take life far too seriously. (*By now,* VICTOR *has crossed to his desk and sat down. He busies himself with the finishing of some letter.*)

VICTOR. Life *is* serious. What man does with life even more so.

HENRY. Have it your way, but there's no need to be pompous. (*The book.*) Perhaps this will cheer you up. A new thesis in biochemistry.

VICTOR. That's your field, not mine.

HENRY. Ah, but this work is by Albertus Magnus. (VICTOR *looks up.*) "Natural Philosophy and Chemical Persuasion." The book is quite fascinating, and Magnus *is* your favorite professor.

VICTOR. He was.

HENRY. You ought to read it. You haven't already purchased it?

VICTOR. No.

HENRY. Good.

VICTOR. Peculiar that you should bring up his name.

HENRY. How so?

VICTOR. I'm finishing a letter to him.

HENRY. Indeed.

VICTOR. I'm informing him that I do not intend to return to Ingolstadt.

HENRY. You mean, until you've regained your health.

VICTOR. I mean—never. (HENRY *moves to Downstage chair, sits in such a way that his body is angled to face* VICTOR *at the desk.*)

HENRY. Victor, is this because of your brother?

VICTOR. (*Thoughtfully.*) I confess William's murder is not a thing I accept easily. To live less than ten years when life holds out so much promise, and die at the hands of an unknown killer, seems to me the height of cosmic cruelty.

HENRY. Cosmic cruelty? The lad was murdered for an expensive gold cross. Obviously by a thief of the lowest kind. Vicious and unfeeling. A monster.

MOTHER'S VOICE. (*From Off Up Right.*) Victor, may I come in?

VICTOR. It's my mother. Please do not make any mention of William. She holds up extremely well, but—

HENRY. I understand. (VICTOR *rises, takes out a chain of keys, moves Up Center.*)

VICTOR. One moment, Mother. I'll unlock the door. (VICTOR *exits.* HENRY *opens the book, reads.* FRAU FRANKENSTEIN, VICTOR's *mother, enters Up Center.* HENRY *stands.*)

MOTHER. Ah, Henry, how wonderful that you're here. (HENRY *bows politely.*)

HENRY. Always a pleasure, Frau Frankenstein. (VICTOR *enters Up Center.*)

MOTHER. I can't tell you what your visits mean to Victor. You, his best friend, have never deserted him.

HENRY. Boys together, friends together. Comrades always.

MOTHER. Did you hear that, Victor?

VICTOR. I have never doubted Henry's friendship. As I trust he will never doubt mine.

MOTHER. (*Sits on sofa.*) If you could only persuade him to get out and around. My son does nothing but lock himself here in the study as if the sound of another human voice was more than he could bear.

VICTOR. You exaggerate, Mother. (*He moves behind the sofa.*)

MOTHER. No, Victor, I do not. (*To Henry.*) He never sleeps. Sophie is at her wits' end trying to think of something that will tease his appetite. Elizabeth has become his devoted nurse, but I'm afraid my son is a bad patient. (*Takes* VICTOR's *hand.*) I do worry about you. The doctor says—

VICTOR. (*Scoffs.*) The doctor—

MOTHER. You shouldn't scoff like that, Victor. You're a scientific man yourself.

VICTOR. There is a world of difference, Mother, between a doctor and a scientific man.

MOTHER. If there is I'm not aware of it. I only meant that you shouldn't insult him by your indifference. He has your best interests at heart. You know you can't go on the way you have. You must eat, rest. (*Angrily,* VICTOR *pulls his hand away, turns his back.*)

VICTOR. Oh, stop it, Mother. (HENRY *and* FRAU FRANKENSTEIN *exchange an embarrassed look.*)

HENRY. (*Eager to change the subject.*) And where is Elizabeth this fine day?

MOTHER. She went to the flower market. I believe she could live her life there. But she was that way even as a child. She could tell you the name of any flower that grew. Victor could pull a flower apart and tell you exactly what was inside of it, what made it grow.

HENRY. Some would find that an ideal combination. The pragmatic and the romantic.

MOTHER. (*Thinks.*) Yes, yes. That's very good, Henry. Very good, indeed. (SOPHIE *has entered Up Center.*)

SOPHIE. I'm sorry to disturb you, Frau Frankenstein.

MOTHER. What is it, Sophie?

SOPHIE. It's Ernst Hessler. (HENRY, VICTOR *and* MOTHER *tense.*)

VICTOR. I'll see him outside. (VICTOR *moves toward Up Center exit, is stopped by:*)

MOTHER. No, Victor. (*To* SOPHIE.) Show him in here, Sophie. (SOPHIE *nods, exits.*)

HENRY. Perhaps I should leave.

MOTHER. Nonsense. It's probably something quite routine about . . . the investigation.

VICTOR. I don't think you should see him. You know how upset you get.

MOTHER. Victor, it is you who gets upset. (*A second passes and* SOPHIE *again appears Up Center.*)

SOPHIE. Inspector General Hessler. (ERNST *enters Up Center, moves to* FRAU FRANKENSTEIN.)

ERNST. I am sorry to intrude, Frau Frankenstein.

MOTHER. You are always welcome in my house, Ernst. (*She holds out her hand. He kisses it in a perfunctory manner.*) You know Henry, of course. Our neighbor.

ERNST. (*Slight bow.*) Herr Clerval. (*To* VICTOR.) Victor. (VICTOR *nods.*)

MOTHER. You'll stay for tea?

ERNST. I'm afraid not.

VICTOR. Then this is a professional visit?

ERNST. Yes.

MOTHER. Something . . . something about William's . . . murder? (ERNST *looks to* HENRY.) Henry is a dear and trusted friend of this family. You may speak freely in front of him.

ERNST. As you wish. (*To business.*) We have William's cross. (*Takes it from some pocket. All react.*)

VICTOR. Who had it?

ERNST. A girl by the name of Justine tried to sell it in Geneva. Unfortunately for her, the buyer was one of our informants.

HENRY. A girl?

ERNST. A bad sort. She travels with horse dealers. Gypsies. Her kind would cut a throat for a tablespoon.

MOTHER. (*Repulsed.*) Please.

ERNST. An unfortunate choice of words. Forgive me.

VICTOR. There can be no mistake?

ERNST. They were encamped on the lake shore the day of William's murder. We know your brother visited the encampment. He was seen there. It's a popular spot for local boys. The girl was seen talking to him, admiring the cross at his neck. The night of the murder the gypsies broke camp and moved on.

HENRY. Hardly seems sufficient to prove this girl guilty.

ERNST. She has a bad record. We have her on file.

MOTHER. She has confessed?

ERNST. Far from it. She denies any knowledge of the crime.

MOTHER. If that is so, how can you be so positive?

ERNST. Because of the absurd story she made up to cover her deed.

VICTOR. What story?

ERNST. She claims a man gave her the cross.

HENRY. Is that so extraordinary?

ERNST. Ah, but this man was no ordinary mortal. He was large and stitched together like a rag doll.

VICTOR. *What!*

ERNST. She had the impudence to offer that myth to me. I thought I heard them all, but a large man stitched together was a new one.

VICTOR. *No!*

MOTHER. Victor, are you all right?

VICTOR. (*To* ERNST *crossing to the French doors.*) Why did you have to bring this news?

ERNST. It is my duty. I assure you, Victor, I had no idea it would upset you in this manner.

MOTHER. (*Stands.*) My son has been under a doctor's care. He's not himself at all. Forgive him.

VICTOR. (*To* ERNST.) Get out.

HENRY. Victor, get a hold of yourself.

VICTOR. *Get out, I said.* (ERNST *bows to* VICTOR, *nods to* HENRY.)

MOTHER. I'll see you to the door.

ERNST. Thank you, Frau Frankenstein. (*She leads the way.*)

MOTHER. I wonder, Ernst, might I have the cross?

ERNST. I'm afraid not. Evidence.

MOTHER. I understand.

ERNST. When the case is closed, I'll see that it's returned. (*She glances nervously at* VICTOR. MOTHER *and* ERNST *are out.* HENRY *stands.*)

HENRY. Was that necessary? If you go on this way,

there's nothing ahead but disaster for you. You've got to take the doctor's advice.

VICTOR. Did you believe him?

HENRY. The doctor?

VICTOR. (*Bitterly.*) No, not the doctor. Ernst. What he said about that girl's story.

HENRY. I have not reason not to believe him.

VICTOR. "Stitched together like a rag doll."

HENRY. The girl was lying.

VICTOR. Was she?

HENRY. It's as simple as that—a lie. Nothing more.

VICTOR. I assure you even simplicity can turn into something twisted and evil. Today's exhilaration can fade quickly into tomorrow's grief.

HENRY. (*Irritated by* VICTOR's *gloominess.*) Can't you say a single sentence without decorating it with crepe?

VICTOR. (*Directly.*) The girl was not lying.

HENRY. Be reasonable.

VICTOR. (*Furious.*) Don't patronize me! I tell you the girl spoke the truth.

HENRY. I will not stand here and listen to this raving. (HENRY *moves to the Up Center exit.*)

VICTOR. (*Distraught.*) Henry, if our friendship means anything at all. I ask you to stay. I plead with you to stay.

HENRY. (*Turns.*) On one condition.

VICTOR. What is that?

HENRY. The Victor Frankenstein who left this chateau for the university was not the same man who returned here for sanctuary as you call it. Something happened to him during that time he was gone. I want to know what it was, and unless you are prepared to tell me of your affliction—

VICTOR. (*Cutting him off.*) Yes, yes. I intend to. I want to. I must. (*Moves to him.*) You are my last hope. What I am going to tell you will chill the marrow of your mortal bones.

HENRY. Let me be the judge of whether or not my 'mortal bones' will freeze. (*Quickly,* VICTOR *crosses to the desk and from some drawer pulls a ledger, various papers and documents.*)

VICTOR. If I appear unsettled and half-mad, there is a reason.

HENRY. If you're referring to Ernst's visit I can only comment that it is unjust to blame the messenger for the message.

VICTOR. You think that's why I cried out?

HENRY. What else am I to think?

VICTOR. (*Points to ledger, papers, etc.*) The secret of my unrest lies here. In these documents and papers. The recorded crimes of Victor Frankenstein. (VICTOR *moves toward the center of the room. Curious,* HENRY *crosses to the desk and looks over the material. Eventually,* HENRY *sits behind the desk.* VICTOR *moves about for the best stage picture as he speaks.*) You think that whatever happened began at the university. You are wrong. (*Points to laboratory door.*) It began behind that laboratory door. As a boy, science and biology consumed me, as it did you—far more than the fever that now plagues my brain. I was more advanced in my studies than even you realized. The university merely stimulated me to press on into the secret that has baffled men from the moment they first sucked breath.

HENRY. What secret?

VICTOR. I often asked myself from where did the principle of life proceed?

HENRY. A bold question.

VICTOR. Yet we are always on the brink of discovering something new and strange and bold. Our cowardice or carelessness defeat us. We restrain our inquiries in fear of what we might discover. We fear the unknown and long to embrace it. I had one passion and only one. To examine the causes of life. And to do that I first had to have recourse to death.

HENRY. Death?

VICTOR. I became acquainted with the science of anatomy in a way that was zealous, accelerated. I observed the natural decay and corruption of the human body.

HENRY. In the dissecting room of the university, you mean. (*As* VICTOR *is speaking, his passion and emotional involvement is painfully obvious. He rants, he gestures, he pauses, he speaks clearly, intelligently, per-suasively. Always, with his words, there is the awesome realization that what he speaks might be true and this horror is conveyed to* HENRY, *who listens in a state of morbid fascination.*)

VICTOR. (*Contemptuous.*) No, I do not mean in the dissecting room of the university.

HENRY. What do you mean, then?

VICTOR. I mean that the charnel-house became my haunt. I lived with the stench of decay in my nostrils. A church graveyard was not a holy place to me. It was, instead, only the receptacle of bodies deprived of life.

HENRY. I don't believe it.

VICTOR. Then you are a fool. I saw how the fine form of man was degraded and wasted. I beheld the corruption of death and studied until my senses no longer knew the hour, the day, the week. And finally in the midst of my darkness a sudden light broke in upon me —a light so brilliant and wondrous, yet so simple, that while I became dizzy with the prospect of success, I was surprised that among so many men of genius I alone, Victor Frankenstein, should be reserved to discover so astonishing a secret.

HENRY. (*Annoyed with* VICTOR's *mood.*) That again.

VICTOR. I asked for your friendship, not your skepticism.

HENRY. You have both. Go on.

VICTOR. The stages of the discovery were distinct and probable. Others could have discovered what I did. Albertus Magnus, for one. But brilliant minds must match their gifts with boldness and imagination, not be earthbound by the improbable. After days and nights of incredible labor and fatigue, I succeeded in discovering the cause of generation and life. I was capable of bestowing animation upon lifeless matter.

HENRY. That's not possible, Victor.

VICTOR. (*Laughs.*) You think not? You, too, are earthbound. When I found so astonishing a power placed within my hands, I hesitated a long time before I decided how to employ it.

HENRY. And how did you?

VICTOR. (*Flat, unemotional.*) I began the creation of a human being.

HENRY. (*Incredulous.*) You did what? (VICTOR *sits, half-enjoying his dreadful recollection and the effect it's having on* HENRY.)

VICTOR. In a solitary chamber at the top of my rooming house, I kept a workshop of filthy creation.

HENRY. (*Stands.*) How could you "create" another human being?

VICTOR. With considerable dedication and a strong stomach. The city morgue and the charity hospital furnished my materials. From one, I stole a hand. From another, I purchased a leg. On dark nights the graveyard proved productive in direct proportion to the energy I was willing to expend in opening a grave.

HENRY. No more, Victor! Enough!

VICTOR. I became nervous to a painful degree. The fall of a leaf startled me, and I shunned everyone as if I were guilty of a crime. I collected the instruments of life around my table, and when I finished I fell asleep across my cot, troubled by dreams.

HENRY. (*Moves toward him.*) I should think so. And that was the end of your experiment?

VICTOR. If only it could have been. I dreamed I saw the grave worms crawling in the folds of my father's funeral shroud. I startled from my sleep in horror, and I beheld the life I created with these hands staring down at me, one hand outstretched as if the Creature

were imploring some aid. (*Deep breath.*) There. Now
you know.

HENRY. (*Convinced* VICTOR *is insane.*) I know what
you have told me.

VICTOR. You still don't understand?

HENRY. What more can there be?

VICTOR. Ernst . . . William's murder . . . the gypsy
girl. Think, Henry, think. (*Recalls* ERNST's *words.*)
"Ah, but this man was no ordinary mortal. He was
large and stitched together like a rag doll." It was he,
my Creature, made from the bits and pieces of other
men, who murdered little William. (*Rises, seizes* HENRY
by the shoulders.) Don't you understand? He's found
me! He's followed me here to Geneva.

HENRY. If what you say is true, why would he do
that? Why would he murder William? Why would he
hate you? You gave him life. No, it's too preposterous.

VICTOR. You must listen!

HENRY. (*Breaking away.*) I've heard more than
enough.

VICTOR. I'm not mad!

HENRY. (*Exits Up Center.*) You will be if you continue this way.

VICTOR. Henry! (*He moves after him.*) I asked for
your help. Do not desert me! (*Suddenly,* VICTOR *freezes.
It's as if a cold wind has blown across his heart. Afraid,
he turns and sees the* CREATURE [*see production notes*],
*who has entered via the open French doors, standing
inside the room, his arms outstretched as if to embrace
the horrified Frankenstein.*) Henry, Henry! (*Turns to*
CREATURE.) Devil! Murderer! (CREATURE *takes a step
toward his creator.* HENRY *returns, sees* CREATURE, *reacts.* VICTOR *backs away.*) Do you still doubt me? See
for yourself. Stitched together like a demon from hell.
Here standing before you is the proof of my infamy!
(HENRY *can't accept it. He's too shocked for any action.*)

HENRY. God help you, Victor. (*Then:*) God help us all.

CREATURE. (*Slowly, dramatically, an emotional appeal.*) Frankenstein . . . help *me*.

CURTAIN

ACT ONE

SCENE 2

AT RISE: *Night. Drapes have been drawn across the French doors, giving the study a "closed in" feeling. Lamps glow. The* CREATURE *is seated in the Downstage chair, which has been turned around to face the audience squarely. The anatomy chart has been placed beside the* CREATURE. HENRY, *in shirtsleeves, is examining him. He's wildly excited.*

HENRY. (*Moving the* CREATURE'S *head from side to side.*) . . . And to the best of your knowledge, you had no adverse reaction to the anaesthetic?

CREATURE. No.

HENRY. No paralysis of any kind?

CREATURE. No. (HENRY *moves to the desk and makes some notes. He picks up a measuring tape or something similar and returns to the* CREATURE. *First he studies the chart and, then, he proceeds to take head measurements.*)

HENRY. I'm rather amazed about the eyelids. Moist, lubricated by circulating the tears. And the cornea—clear, transparent. The membrane functions normally. Stand up, please. (*The* CREATURE *obeys.*) Run in place. (*The* CREATURE *begins to run in place, fast.*) No, no, no. Slowly. (*The* CREATURE *slows down.*) Excellent. You may be seated. (HENRY *returns to the desk and picks up a paper weight, crosses back to the* CREATURE, *hands it to him.*) I want to test the strength of your grip. (*The* CREATURE *holds out the paper weight and proceeds to crush it with ease. See Production Notes.* HENRY *is amazed, takes back the weight and places it on the desk.*) I would say the end results are not yet cosmetically satisfactory, and there is a decided tendency toward hyperthydroidism, but in all other respects you are remarkable. I would have thought if such an experiment succeeded the conclusion would be a chronic invalid. (*More notes.*) I was wrong for doubting Victor.

CREATURE. Is that all I am?

HENRY. How do you mean?

CREATURE. An experiment.

HENRY. (*Puts down his notes.*) Far more than an experiment, my strange friend. You are living proof that worn out parts can be replaced. You offer hope for an extended life span. (VICTOR *enters from laboratory, putting on his jacket. He stands listening, unobserved by the* CREATURE.)

CREATURE. I am a monster. A living thing that is dead. I am alone, lonely. All men shun Frankenstein's creation.

VICTOR. And why shouldn't they? Murderer.

HENRY. Did you sleep at all?

VICTOR. I never sleep. Not any more. All I do is dream of horrors. (VICTOR *sits on the sofa.*)

HENRY. (*Crosses to* VICTOR.) This is no horror. Whatever your technique, you have opened a special field of surgical study.

VICTOR. (*Unimpressed.*) If one is a sadistic vivisectionist.

HENRY. He has the power of locomotion. Complete mastery of speech, reasoning, deduction. His parts will not wear out.

VICTOR. A living machine.

HENRY. Yes, if you will.

VICTOR. Beware, Henry. The excitement in your voice betrays you. You have caught my fever. (HENRY *crosses to the* CREATURE.)

HENRY. No extra fingers, no missing cartilage. Blood pulsates through his veins as it does through yours and mine.

VICTOR. Blood of dead men.

HENRY. (*Insistent.*) This is *no* monster. You have engineered a finely tooled machine powered by an intricate network of muscles and tendons. The grafting is amateurish, repulsive, but it suffices.

VICTOR. You have forgotten something.

HENRY. I shouldn't wonder.

VICTOR. (*Stands.*) There sits the hideous "thing" that has come to kill me.

CREATURE. That is no longer true.

VICTOR. I curse the day I gave you life.

CREATURE. I expected this reception. All men hate the wretched. How I must be hated then. I am miserable beyond all living things. I did not always hate you, Victor Frankenstein. The night you brought me to life, I rushed from your rooms believing the world would welcome me. I thought myself no different than others. I watched you sleeping and saw no great dissimilarity between us.

VICTOR. That is disgusting.

HENRY. No, it is not. You brought him into existence. It is perfectly natural that he would think you and he were both of a kind.

VICTOR. (*Incensed.*) Both of a kind!

CREATURE. I am one of no kind. An outcast. Wherever I showed myself people ran in terror and repulsion. I had no friend. In the winter I froze sleeping in the hills. In the summer I hid in the woods.

HENRY. Were you harmed in any way? Physically, I mean.

CREATURE. Hunters came into the woods searching for game. I had never seen a gun or heard its sound. It frightened me and I ran, but they followed after. (*Touches his shoulder.*) A great pain tore into me, and I saw my own blood for the first time. It sickened me.

HENRY. You hear that, Victor? He felt pain. He knows fear.

VICTOR. As I do. As you should. (*To* CREATURE.) Go from this house. Leave me.

CREATURE. Have I not suffered enough? Now you seek to increase my misery?

VICTOR. Is that why you have sought me out? To come here for a hiding place? Is that why you murdered a defenseless boy?

CREATURE. (*Stands.*) I did not murder him. You did, Frankenstein. (VICTOR *stiffens.* HENRY *moves toward the desk, watching the duo confront one another.*)

VICTOR. You dare say that to me?

CREATURE. A creature such as I must dare. I saw a child coming toward me. Suddenly, as I gazed on him, an idea seized me that this little creature had lived too short a time to understand the horror of deformity. If I could educate him before others imparted their prejudice, I should not be so desolate in this peopled earth. I would not be alone. For of all curses, that is the one I loathe above all others.

HENRY. (*Curious more than accusative.*) But why murder?

CREATURE. I had no such intention. At first. I seized him as he passed. As soon as he beheld my form, he placed his hands before his eyes and uttered a shrill cry. "Let me go!" he screamed. "Monster! Ugly wretch! Let me go or I will tell Victor. He will punish you! Victor Frankenstein, my brother, will punish you!"

VICTOR. (*Visibly shaken.*) Poor, poor William.

CREATURE. I swelled with hellish triumph. I thought, I, too, can create desolation. My enemy is not invulnerable. This death will carry despair to him, and a thousand other miseries shall torment and destroy him. Frankenstein will suffer as I have suffered. (HENRY *and* VICTOR *say nothing for a moment and, then, the* CREATURE *sits.*) Have you suffered, Frankenstein?

VICTOR. More than I would have thought possible.

CREATURE. Then I am satisfied. You have created me, but your work is not finished.

VICTOR. It is . . . finished.

CREATURE. You have created me. You must destroy me.

HENRY. (*Alarmed.*) What!

VICTOR. (*A thoughtful pause.*) We are in accord. At last.

CREATURE. Then you'll do it?

VICTOR. Yes.

HENRY. Victor!

CREATURE. When?

VICTOR. Tonight.

HENRY. Victor, I protest. (VICTOR's *manner is efficient and direct. The unemotional scientist. He crosses to the laboratory door, opens it.*)

VICTOR. We can't risk having you seen. You'll be safe in there until I'm ready. Make no sound. (*The* CREATURE *stands, crosses for the laboratory.*)

CREATURE. Remember this—my agony is greater than yours. (*The* CREATURE *enters the laboratory.*)

VICTOR. No one ever goes in there. But to be safe . . . (VICTOR *locks the door.*)

HENRY. You cannot be serious about his request.

VICTOR. Ah, but I am. He has brought me my salvation. (*As they discourse,* VICTOR *goes to the drapes masking the French doors, opens them. Early morning sun streams in.*)

HENRY. It would be murder.

VICTOR. You cannot murder a walking inventory of borrowed human parts.

HENRY. That's absurd and you know it.

VICTOR. Call it anything you like. Execution, a balancing of the scales. Retribution, if you will. Anything but murder. There is blood on my hands for having created him.

HENRY. And you think that by destroying him you can wash away that blood. Is that it?

VICTOR. It is my only hope.

HENRY. Then I appeal to you as a man of science. I do not speak now as a dear friend. I speak to you as another who is dedicated to pushing back the barriers of ignorance.

VICTOR. Barriers? (*Points to laboratory door.*) I crumbled one barrier and look at the result.

HENRY. I have looked and what I've found is both miraculous and marvelous. This "creature" is not at fault. He was an innocent thrust into a world that has no comfortable place for the unordinary. He had every right to expect gentleness and understanding. Instead, he found that mankind itself is very often monstrous.

VICTOR. There is nothing you can say that I haven't said to myself a hundred times. (*Crosses to desk, grabs some photograph, moves to* HENRY, *puts the frame into his hand.*) Here, look into the face of William. You speak of an innocent. There is your innocent. My young brother.

HENRY. Victor, be sensible. I am speaking to your intellect, not your emotion.

VICTOR. Damn your intellect.

HENRY. And damn your emotion! (*From Off—Up Right.*)

MOTHER'S VOICE. Victor, Victor?

VICTOR. (*Takes out his keys.*) Say nothing of this. To anyone.

HENRY. For the time being.

VICTOR. Return this evening. I will need your assistance.

MOTHER'S VOICE. Victor? (VICTOR *exits Up Center with the key ready to unlock the hallway door.* HENRY *moves to the desk and puts down the framed photograph.*) I shan't hear another word. If you will not come to the breakfast table, you shall eat in the study. (*By now, she has entered.* VICTOR *stands Left of Up Center entrance.* MOTHER *wears an attractive robe over her nightgown.*) Henry? Here so early?

HENRY. I'm afraid I never left.

MOTHER. (*Sees anatomy chart, disorder on the desk. She sighs protectively.*) I was counting on you to help Victor *rest*. And look at this. It's as if you were boys again. Up all night with your studies and vile smelling test tubes. You'll stay for breakfast?

HENRY. Sleep at the moment is more appealing than nourishment.

MOTHER. I shall be angry with you if you encourage Victor in any work. It would be quite destructive.

HENRY. (*Meaning the* CREATURE.) I agree with you. If you'll excuse me? (*Takes his jacket from some chair, puts it on.*) It's a lovely day outside. I'll enjoy the walk home. I have a great deal to think about. Until later, Victor. (*At French doors.*) Frau Frankenstein. (MOTHER *nods,* HENRY *exits.* VICTOR *moves Down Center.*)

MOTHER. (*Touches his face.*) If you could see your eyes. I can count every tiny vein.

VICTOR. I would like to be alone, Mother.

MOTHER. No, Victor. I have given in to your whims and ways far too often. Elizabeth is taking you into the city this morning. She has shopping to do.

VICTOR. You think that interests me? Shopping!

MOTHER. No, I'm sure the shopping will bore you, but Elizabeth's company will be pleasant. (*He turns away.*) Won't it? (SOPHIE *enters Up Center with a breakfast tray.*) Ah, Sophie. Good, good. Put the tray on Victor's desk.

VICTOR. I am *not* hungry. (MOTHER *ignores him. Moves the anatomy chart back to its proper position.*)

MOTHER. I am going to insist that you allow Sophie in here to clean.

SOPHIE. I haven't been in here for so long, Herr Frankenstein. Everything is covered with dust. It's not healthy to breathe dust.

VICTOR. Is that your medical opinion?

MOTHER. There is no need to be rude.

VICTOR. I have asked that you respect my wishes. Do not enter unless the door is unlocked.

MOTHER. You allow Henry to come and go at will through the garden.

VICTOR. That is another matter.

MOTHER. Neither Sophie, Elizabeth nor I have ever bothered you about your laboratory. Although, at times, the smells have been unbearable. However, other people do come into the study. You're not being fair. Let Sophie clean.

VICTOR. (*Sits on sofa, resigned.*) If only all matters could be reduced to such elements. To eat a breakfast, to go shopping, to clean a room.

MOTHER. (*Trying to pull him from the doldrums.*) Sophie has a surprise for you. (*She crosses back to the chair in which the* CREATURE *was sitting, puts it back into position.*)

SOPHIE. Strawberries. First of the season, Herr Frankenstein.

VICTOR. Leave the tray.

MOTHER. Sophie, bring me the strawberries. (*SOPHIE picks up the bowl, crosses to* MOTHER, *hands her the bowl.*) Eat the strawberries, Victor. (*He laughs.*) Is that so amusing?

VICTOR. Mother . . . you're so good . . . so comforting . . . strawberries. Strawberries! (*He laughs again.* MOTHER *and* SOPHIE *exchange an amazed look and they, too, get caught in* VICTOR's *mood and join in.* ELIZABETH *enters Up Center dressed most attractively. She carries a hat box, looks at the laughing trio, amazed.*)

ELIZABETH. (*Bright smile.*) I'm sorry I wasn't here a moment earlier. I like a good joke as well as the next.

VICTOR. (*Smiling.*) Not that, not that at all. It's just that I was struck by the incongruity of my dark moods and my mother's dish of strawberries.

SOPHIE. They're perfectly good strawberries, sir. The

man who sold them to me is reliable. I've never had any complaints about his produce.

VICTOR. I'm sure you haven't. (*He takes the strawberries and begins to eat. The women are delighted.*) Delicious.

MOTHER. (*Sigh of relief.*) Come along, Sophie. We'll leave them alone. (SOPHIE *starts out, followed by* MOTHER, *who turns Up Center.*) And you will let Sophie clean in here?

VICTOR. (*Eating.*) Yes, yes.

MOTHER. When, dear?

VICTOR. (*Anxious to close the subject.*) Soon. (MOTHER *gives a gesture of resignation to* ELIZABETH, *exits.* ELIZABETH *moves to some table, or the desk, and puts down the hat box.*)

ELIZABETH. (*The breakfast tray.*) I put the bud vase on the tray myself. Did you notice the petals?

VICTOR. No. What is the flower?

ELIZABETH. There isn't any. I only wanted to see if you'd notice.

VICTOR. (*Puts down the dish.*) I have been insensitive, haven't I?

ELIZBETH. I understand. No one here but solicitous women who would smother you with trivialities and fresh strawberries.

VICTOR. Most men would find that an enviable condition. (ELIZABETH *opens the hat box, takes out a wedding veil.*)

ELIZABETH. I can't make up my mind about this veil. I thought we might return it to the shop and see what else they had.

VICTOR. Not a subtle hint.

ELIZABETH. Victor, listen to me. I don't pretend I'm not disturbed by your strange moods and temperament. You're different from other men, true. Perhaps that's the very quality that attracts me. We've grown up together and I have always loved you. I don't know what troubles you. You're complex and difficult. I'm not blind to that. But, Victor, don't close your heart to me. Don't keep your love from me.

VICTOR. If only I could be honest.

ELIZABETH. (*Crosses to him, puts the veil on sofa.*) I want to help you in life. I want to be with you. We were companions as children. We'll be companions now. Only closer, dearer.

VICTOR. (*Recites the cliche with an almost hopeful smile.*) And you'll read to me, and cook for me, and comfort me when I'm alone and others might turn against me?

ELIZABETH. Don't make light of such things, Victor. They count for something. I would do all those things. Gladly.

VICTOR. Then a wife is truly a wonderful thing.

ELIZABETH. Let me be wonderful for you, Victor. I have never loved anyone else. I never shall. You will never be alone. I promise you that. (VICTOR *stands, takes her hand, kisses it.*)

VICTOR. Dear, dear Elizabeth.

ELIZABETH. (*Happily.*) Come along now . . . we'll have the morning together. We'll visit the flower market. (VICTOR *seems to brighten.*)

VICTOR. My dark moods will soon be at an end. And I promise you that, Elizabeth. Yes, yes, by all means— the flower market. (ELIZABETH *holds out her hand and* VICTOR *crosses to her and they sweep out the French doors, delighted in each other's company. A moment passes and, then, the door to the laboratory opens. In her happiness,* ELIZABETH *has forgotten the bridal veil. The* CREATURE *has obviously been eavesdropping. He moves to the sofa and picks up the veil. He finds it a thing of wonder and pleasure. Over and over in his hands he turns it, as if he almost expected it to change shape. Tenderly, lovingly, he caresses it to his cheek.*)

CREATURE. (*Smiles in anticipation.*) Wife.

CURTAIN

ACT ONE

Scene 3

At Rise: *That evening. Drapes are drawn at Up Center. At the French doors, the drapes are pulled to the sides revealing a moonlit night, one door open. Victor is at his desk, poring over books and assorted notes, a lamp burning beside him. He works at a feverish pace, checking and re-checking, making notations in his ledgers. He wears a white smock.*

Victor. (*Barely audible.*) . . . The bronchial tubes and then into the chest cavity . . . the tendons and the attached muscle and tissues . . . the large veins into the muscular structure of the heart . . . no resuturing required . . . totally sever the arm . . . the leg . . . complete reversal of transplantation . . . (*The Creature quietly comes from the laboratory and stands watching Victor. The scientist is wholly preoccupied and is unaware of the intrusion.*) . . . the spinal column compressed . . . no attempt to minimize of the loss of blood to brain tissue . . . yes, yes . . .

Creature. Frankenstein.

Victor. (*Looks up.*) It won't be long now. You shall have your wish. I'm waiting for Henry. I'll need his assistance.

Creature. How will you do it?

Victor. I put you together piece by piece. Your whole anatomical structure is a patchwork of transplanted blood vessels, tissues, bones. I shall simply reverse the process. You will cease to exist piece by piece. You needn't worry. I'll attack the brain first. You'll feel nothing.

Creature. And the "pieces."

Victor. The disposal of the "pieces" is not the concern of surgery. Still, if you must know—

Creature. (*Interrupts.*) Yes . . . tell me

VICTOR. Several options. Quicklime . . . acid . . . burial.

CREATURE. None of those, Frankenstein.

VICTOR. You have something else in mind?

CREATURE. I will live.

VICTOR. (*Doesn't understand.*) No, you will not live. Once the surgery is finished you will be *erased* from this earth.

CREATURE. (*Repeats.*) I will live, Frankenstein.

VICTOR. What the devil do you mean?

CREATURE. I have a passion which you alone can gratify.

VICTOR. I have vowed to grant your request. Tonight your agony ends and my life begins anew.

CREATURE. No, Frankenstein. *My* life begins anew. (VICTOR *slowly rises, moves in front of his desk.*)

VICTOR. What are you saying?

CREATURE. We will not part until you grant my wish.

VICTOR. You wish for more than death?

CREATURE. Yes. More than death. Life. This time not for me, but for another.

VICTOR. Another?

CREATURE. I am alone and miserable.

VICTOR. Tonight I end that misery.

CREATURE. Men will not associate with me, but one as deformed and horrible as myself would not deny herself to me. My companion must be of the same species and have the same defects as I.

VICTOR. No such creature exists.

CREATURE. You must create her. (VICTOR *is struck dumb, he leans back against the desk for support.*)

VICTOR. I thought you sought oblivion.

CREATURE. What I ask of you is reasonable and moderate.

VICTOR. Reasonable!

CREATURE. I demand one of another sex, but as hideous as myself. I demand a *bride* for Frankenstein's creature.

VICTOR. You *demand*. You have no right to demand anything of me.

CREATURE. If you consent neither you nor any other human being shall ever see us again.

VICTOR. (*His hands to his ears.*) I won't listen.

CREATURE. You must create a female for me with whom I can live in companionship. This you alone can do, and I demand it of you as a right which you must not refuse.

VICTOR. *I do refuse!*

CREATURE. Do not incite my anger.

VICTOR. I do not fear your anger, and no torture shall ever extort a consent from me.

CREATURE. Is what I ask so difficult?

VICTOR. For me it is an impossibility. You ask me to create another like yourself.

CREATURE. I do.

VICTOR. Two whose joint wickedness might desolate the world.

CREATURE. We will harm no living thing.

VICTOR. How did you come by this preposterous idea?

CREATURE. By listening to one who loves you.

VICTOR. (*Understands.*) So you were listening at the door when I spoke with Elizabeth.

CREATURE. Her words were gentle.

VICTOR. I have agreed to give you death. By the hands that were responsible for giving you life. Beyond that, I owe you nothing.

CREATURE. Reconsider.

VICTOR. Never.

CREATURE. You are wrong and instead of threatening, I am content to reason with you.

VICTOR. You are malicious.

CREATURE. I am malicious because I am miserable. You, my creator, would tear me to pieces and triumph. Remember that. And tell me why I should pity man more than he pities me. Shall I respect man when he condemns me? Let him live with me in the interchange of kindness, and instead of injury I would bestow every benefit upon him with tears of gratitude at his acceptance. Why cannot that be, Frankenstein?

VICTOR. Human sensibilities forbid it.

CREATURE. Do as I ask. (VICTOR *turns his back*.) If I cannot inspire, I will cause fear, and chiefly toward you, my enemy. I will revenge my injuries. Have a care. I will work at your destruction, so that you shall curse the hour of your birth.

VICTOR. (*Turns back*.) There! Your true nature. Threatening, dangerous, wicked. Your bride would be a monster, too.

CREATURE. It is true we shall be monsters, cut off from all the world; but on that account we shall be more attached to one another.

VICTOR. What happiness could there be in your lives?

CREATURE. Our lives will not be happy, but they will be harmless and free from the misery I now feel. My creator, let me feel gratitude towards you for one benefit. Let me see that I excite the sympathy of some existing thing. Do not deny me my request. I do not ask of you, Frankenstein. I *beg* of you. (VICTOR *is visibly shaken. He moves to the Downstage chair, sits*.)

VICTOR. There . . . there is some justice in your argument.

CREATURE. We will go to the forest or some jungle. My food is not that of man. I do not destroy the animals to glut my appetite. Acorns and berries will sustain us.

VICTOR. The noble savage.

CREATURE. Do not mock me.

VICTOR. And do not tempt me. (CREATURE *can sense* VICTOR *is weakening*.)

CREATURE. We shall make our bed of dried leaves. The sun will shine on us as on man. Pitiless as you have been towards me, I now see compassion in your eyes.

VICTOR. (*A plea for help.*) Why did you have to return?

CREATURE. I swear to you, by the earth which I inhabit, and by you that made me, that with the companion you bestow I will leave the neighborhood of man forever.

VICTOR. That is what you say now, but what guarantee have I that you would not return, more demanding, stronger than ever before?

CREATURE. With another such as I my evil passions and anger will have fled.

VICTOR. Because you will have a bride?

CREATURE. (*Deeply felt.*) Because I will have sympathy.

VICTOR. Forgive me for having created you.

CREATURE. It is too late for forgiveness. Grant me my wish. My life will flow quietly away, and in my dying moments, when that time comes, I shall not curse my maker. (*The* CREATURE *moves to* VICTOR *and puts his hand on* VICTOR's *shoulder. He stiffens, but is not repulsed at this moment.*)

VICTOR. As your maker, perhaps . . . perhaps . . . I do owe you some measure of . . . happiness.

CREATURE. We shall be things of whose existence everyone will be ignorant. The love of another will destroy the cause of my crimes. Pity me, Victor Frankenstein. Pity me. (*VICTOR is lost in deep thought. The* CREATURE *moves back to the laboratory, turns once to stare at the scientist, exits.* VICTOR *remains seated. Alone, troubled. He stands, paces a few steps.* HENRY *enters via the French doors.*)

HENRY. I'm here as you requested—if only to dissuade you.

VICTOR. (*Turns slowly.*) Always the man of science. Right, Henry?

HENRY. In this matter, yes.

VICTOR. You could never be as persuasive as my Creature.

HENRY. You look distant. What are you thinking?

VICTOR. Paradise Lost.

HENRY. Paradise?

VICTOR. The words of Milton: "Did I request thee, Maker, from my clay/To mould me Man, did I solicit thee/From darkness to promote me?"

HENRY. (*Moves Downstage.*) You gave him life, Victor. And now you want to take it from him.

VICTOR. The Creature has had second thoughts.

HENRY. What do you mean?

VICTOR. Death is no longer to be its destination.

HENRY. He wants to live?

VICTOR. More than that.

HENRY. Surely that's enough.

VICTOR. You don't understand.

HENRY. I'm trying to.

VICTOR. He asks that I create a bride. Yes, a *bride*.

HENRY. (*Impressed.*) He's more human than I realized.

VICTOR. A companion to share his wretched loneliness.

HENRY. But it's . . . it's unthinkable.

VICTOR. Aha! So now Henry Clerval has second thoughts. Yet it was Henry Clerval who sought to dissuade me.

HENRY. Dissuade you from destroying what was already in existence. I couldn't condone murder in any form. But to create a second creature is not the same at all.

VICTOR. Test your fire, Henry. Put your scientific zeal to the crucible. You have marvelled at my "genius." You have been swept up in this bold experiment. You held staunch, while I wavered.

HENRY. For the possibilities the experiment offered.

VICTOR. I cannot do it alone. A second time would be impossible. I must have another with me. The Creature has promised they will live apart from man. Quietly. Without maliciousness.

HENRY. And if you refuse?

VICTOR. The Creature will become a hound of hell. I will be its prey. (*Change in mood.*) Henry, let us give the creature what it asks. I can't destroy it now, for its appeal was too sincere, springing from its cursed heart.

HENRY. (*Wavering.*) I . . . I don't know . . .

VICTOR. I can compensate for the wickedness of the first by the creation of a gentler second.

HENRY. Perhaps . . .

VICTOR. Help me. If not for the Creature's wish, then for the experiment itself. You were amazed, fascinated. You, alone, among all others will see how the miracle is accomplished. Will you turn your back on that? (HENRY *thinks.*)

HENRY. When would we begin . . . if I agreed?

VICTOR. (*Moves to French doors.*) What better time than tonight? (HENRY *doesn't move.*) Henry, are you not dedicated to pushing back the barriers of ignorance?

HENRY. Where are you going?

VICTOR. Where else? The church graveyard.

HENRY. Graveyard?

VICTOR. (*Cold, detached, scientific.*) It will be m warehouse of spare parts. My salvation, my absoluti I offer you a glimpse of the eternal. The choice is yc

HENRY. (*Pause; then:*) I accept.

VICTOR. Splendid. We'll get shovels from the house. Come along, Henry. (VICTOR *exits in spirits. Caught up in the fever of the adventure moves to follow.*)

FAST CURTAIN

END OF ACT ONE

ACT TWO

Scene 1

TIME: *A week later.*

AT RISE: *The room is in shadows. From behind the laboratory door comes the SOUND of machinery HUMMING. Metallic rumblings coupled with bolts of flashing light that can be glimpsed through cracks in the door give evidence that VICTOR is experimenting with the CREATURE'S bride-to-be. Early morning light, that will FADE UP FULL as the scene progresses, filters in through the French doors. A few seconds more of laboratory activity and, then, SILENCE. Another moment passes and a weary VICTOR enters. He wears a surgical gown, mask, cap. He removes the cap and mask as he crosses to the desk and pours himself a glass of brandy, downs it in a thirsty gulp. HENRY enters via the French doors carrying some wrapped article.*

HENRY. Not too late, am I?

VICTOR. I expected you an hour ago.

HENRY. Couldn't be helped. Any difficulties?

VICTOR. None beyond what we already know. We'll need to increase the voltage.

HENRY. (*Moving in.*) How's he behaving?

VICTOR. More like an expectant father than an expectant groom.

HENRY. Understandable.

VICTOR. He sits in the corner of the laboratory like a huge whipped dog. Watching. If I touch a switch his eyes flick to the spot.

36

HENRY. I've noticed that.

VICTOR. If I rewire the apparatus he takes careful note of how it's done.

HENRY. Testimony to your extraordinary skills.

VICTOR. (*Moves Center.*) Testimony to his craftiness. You've noticed his gift of mimicry. Oh, he watches you, too, Henry. A little while ago I suddenly realized he was unusually quiet.

HENRY. And?

VICTOR. He was studying your notes.

HENRY. My notes?

VICTOR. I think it might be wise if you devised some code or other.

HENRY. If you say so.

VICTOR. It's both touching and horrible to watch him. Whenever I enter the laboratory he's by the surgical table.

HENRY. He never touches anything.

VICTOR. And, yet, he knows every molecule of his bride-to-be. I entered unobserved earlier and found him talking to the incomplete thing.

HENRY. He's never given me a bit of trouble. Undoubtedly, he accepts me as some sort of an apprentice. Nothing more.

VICTOR. Don't be too sure. You've been his champion. He's not likely to forget that.

HENRY. I wonder, Victor, where we would be at this point in our lives if the Creature you created had been beautiful instead of ugly.

VICTOR. Don't mistake me for some kind of moral idiot.

HENRY. You know I don't.

VICTOR. Leave speculations of that sort to philosophy. I don't want you to mistake my full motives. I thought, at one time, a new species would bless me as its creator and source. Many excellent natures would owe their being to me.

HENRY. In one case, at least, that is true.

VICTOR. That monster is far from happy and no-where near excellent.

HENRY. His bride may present a different story.

VICTOR. These experiments with the second Creature intrigue you?

HENRY. Beyond words. You know that. Why do you ask?

VICTOR. You feel no animosity toward him?

HENRY. None. And none to his bride.

VICTOR. Because you're a scientist?

HENRY. Why else?

VICTOR. You wear your badge of scientific inquiry like a coat of arms. Take care it doesn't pierce.

HENRY. I leave gloomy speculation to you, Victor. You're a master.

VICTOR. I suppose. Still, I can't forget easily. When I first saw his terrible eyes looking down upon me in my sleep, I knew I had fallen from the autonomy of a supreme artificer to—

HENRY. To what?

VICTOR. The terror of a child of earth.

HENRY. He is your responsibility. Accept that.

VICTOR. I ran from my responsibility once.

HENRY. Surely you won't do it a second time. We've come too far for such thoughts. I believe him. He wants what he says he wants. He'll never harm another human being.

VICTOR. If only I could share your belief. After all, Henry, it was you who called the murderer of William —"Vicious and unfeeling. A monster."

HENRY. Much too early for intellectual exercises. Unlike you, I look at the birth of this additional Crea-ture from a practical view.

VICTOR. What could be more *im*practical than creat-ing a wife for a Creature that shouldn't exist in the first place? (HENRY *laughs, moves to desk.*)

HENRY. You'll cheer up when you see what I've brought. You don't give yourself enough credit. The safety methods in future surgery that I've learned at your side will help thousands of people. There is a long list of diseases of vital organs for which a healthy transplant would be curative. (HENRY *is carefully unwrapping his bundle.*)

VICTOR. I marvel at your ability to find merit in this enterprise.

HENRY. (*Annoyed.*) And I marvel at your perpetual vacillation. Your self-induced depressions. You love this Creature and you hate him. You have made your bargain. Stick to it.

VICTOR. What have you there?

HENRY. You'll see. Imagine the mercy in replacing a worn out lung with another that is vital and functioning.

VICTOR. In other words, my evil shall henceforth become my good.

HENRY. Think of yourself less a modern Prometheus and more of a humanitarian. (HENRY *crosses to* VICTOR *with the wrapping paper unfolded. We catch a glimpse of a severed human hand.*)

VICTOR. (*Looks, interested.*) Where did you get this one?

HENRY. City morgue. None of the hands so far have been satisfactory.

VICTOR. They were satisfactory, but they weren't fresh. Both aspects are essential.

HENRY. I think this one will do nicely.

VICTOR. Let me have it. (HENRY *passes him the hand.* VICTOR *crosses back to the desk and studies it with the aid of a magnifying glass.*) Hmmmm. Maybe. I can't be positive. The hands from the graveyard all showed signs of congenital defects. We must give her hands where the skin, tendons, muscles, blood vessels and nerves are capable of sustaining sensation and accomplishing motion. (*Closer inspection.*) She couldn't have been dead for long. Good, good.

HENRY. She was young. A derelict.

VICTOR. No questions?

HENRY. The morgue keeper got his price.

VICTOR. I'll want to test for elasticity. (CREATURE *enters from laboratory.*)

HENRY. Victor.

VICTOR. (*Turns.*) I warned you to stay out of sight.

CREATURE. How much longer?

VICTOR. All in good time.

CREATURE. (*Insistent.*) When?

VICTOR. When I decide the time is right.

HENRY. (*To* VICTOR.) Will you name her, or will he?

VICTOR. He can call her whatever he likes.

CREATURE. You must hurry.

VICTOR. Must? Is that a word to use to your creator?

CREATURE. Remember, Frankenstein, I am your creature. I ought to be your Adam.

VICTOR. I see you more as a fallen angel.

HENRY. (*To* CREATURE.) We are doing as you requested.

VICTOR. What more can you want?

CREATURE. Haste.

MOTHER'S VOICE. (*From Off—Up Center.*) Victor?

VICTOR. (*Turns to French doors.*) Morning comes so quickly. (*To* CREATURE.) Stay back. Out of sight. And quiet. (CREATURE *moves to laboratory door, turns.*)

CREATURE. (*The final word.*) Haste. (*He exits.*)

HENRY. I'll make a few more tests. (*He crosses for the door.*)

VICTOR. Henry. (HENRY *turns back.* VICTOR *picks up the wrapping paper with the severed hand.*) Take this with you.

HENRY. Careless of me. (*He takes the hand from* VICTOR, *exits into laboratory.*)

MOTHER'S VOICE. Victor? (VICTOR *doesn't want to admit her, but he has no choice. He takes out his keys, exits Up Center. A moment of silence as* VICTOR *un-*

locks the door.) Why you should prefer to sleep in your laboratory is something I'll never understand.

VICTOR'S VOICE. The cot is comfortable. (*By now both have moved into the study.* MOTHER *moves to sofa.*)

MOTHER. I don't know why I should even bother to be concerned. You ignore my advice in all things.

VICTOR. I'm preoccupied. Is that so difficult to understand?

MOTHER. (*Sits.*) I thought you returned from Ingolstadt because you were exhausted.

VICTOR. I was.

MOTHER. And now?

VICTOR. I'm still exhausted, but the exhaustion is of a different sort.

MOTHER. What rubbish. (*Throws up her hands.*) And what is that supposed to mean—"Exhaustion is of a different sort"?

VICTOR. (*Sitting.*) Mother, I must ask that you leave me to my work.

MOTHER. And what is that work, Victor?

VICTOR. Why do you ask?

MOTHER. Can't I be curious? You're curious. And cautious. You always seem to fear someone will discover a secret about you.

VICTOR. Nonsense.

MOTHER. Delivery men at the door day and night with boxes of who-knows-what. Henry Clerval creeping through the garden at all hours. You think I haven't worried about it all? (*Stands, moves to laboratory.*) The sounds, the lights. What do you hide behind this door, Victor?

VICTOR. Nothing that could possibly interest you.

MOTHER. Let me be the judge. (*She goes to open the door.*)

VICTOR. (*Springs to his feet.*) *No!*

MOTHER. (*Turns, startled.*) What is it? (*Looks at the door and, then, worried, backs off.*) There is something . . . very wrong. Whatever it is you're up to, Victor, it frightens me. (VICTOR *tries to calm the waters.*)

VICTOR. Nothing to be concerned about. You know how I am about my work.

MOTHER. (*Crosses back to him.*) I worry about you. You are the man of this household, Victor, but I can feel you moving farther and farther away from me. (*Sits on sofa again.*) I don't speak much of your brother. I try not to. It was a terrible sorrow when your father died, but I had William and I had my Victor. And, cruelly, William was taken from me. You are the only flesh and blood I have left. (VICTOR *sits beside her.*) Take care not to break my heart. After William, I couldn't stand losing you.

VICTOR. I'm sorry for any pain that I've caused.

MOTHER. You act so unsettled. Angry. (*Then:*) Elizabeth worries, too. She's in love with you. Why do you not marry her?

VICTOR. I love Elizabeth tenderly and sincerely.

MOTHER. Then prove it. Why do you delay?

VICTOR. I've never known anyone who excited my warmest admiration and affection as Elizabeth does.

MOTHER. One might say the same thing about a piece of porcelain.

VICTOR. I mean my words.

MOTHER. I confess, my son, that I have always looked forward to your marriage. It would give me strength in my declining years.

VICTOR. Declining years? You are still a young woman.

MOTHER. You and Elizabeth were attached to one another from your earliest childhood. You studied together and always seemed suited to one another.

VICTOR. What is it you're trying to say?

MOTHER. (*Cautiously.*) I fear, perhaps, you regard her as a sister, without any wish that she might become your wife. (*Sighs, as if a great burden had lifted from her mind.*) There. That is what I fear. (*Almost lightly.*) That and whatever lies behind that laboratory door. (*Concerned.*) Perhaps . . . you may have met another whom you love. Perhaps you consider yourself bound in honor to marry Elizabeth and this brings you pain.

VICTOR. (*Stands.*) I vow to you. My future hopes are entirely bound up with Elizabeth.

MOTHER. (*Stands, faces him.*) If you feel this way about her, marry quickly. And this sullenness which appears to have taken so strong a hold of your mind will dissipate itself. (*Door to laboratory opens and* HENRY, *coatless but wearing a white smock, thunders in. He holds the severed hand in the wrapping paper.*)

HENRY. Victor, it won't do after all. It bruises too easily. (*Sees* MOTHER, *reacts.*) Oh, forgive me, Frau Frankenstein.

MOTHER. What do you have in that wrapping paper? (HENRY *quickly folds the paper around the severed hand.* MOTHER *has seen something, but what she isn't quite certain.*)

HENRY. Oh, uh . . . an idle experiment.

MOTHER. With bruises?

HENRY. It would be of no interest. (MOTHER *can feel the tension in the air.*)

VICTOR. Then I think it would be best if we went into town together. We might "exchange" it for one more suitable.

HENRY. Yes, yes. Good idea. I'll get my coat. (*Returns to laboratory.*)

MOTHER. If you're going shopping, take Elizabeth. She'd enjoy the walk.

VICTOR. This is not a shopping trip. At least, not the kind Elizabeth would appreciate.

MOTHER. If you say so, Victor. (VICTOR *smiles, kisses her on the forehead.*)

VICTOR. Trust me.

MOTHER. I try. (HENRY *returns carrying his jacket.*)

HENRY. I'm ready.

VICTOR. Then we're off. (HENRY *crosses to French doors, putting on his coat, exits.* VICTOR *crosses to the laboratory door and locks it with his key.*)

MOTHER. Will you be back for lunch?

VICTOR. Depends on our trip into town.

MOTHER. You're the despair of Sophie.

VICTOR. And of you, and of Elizabeth, and of Henry, and of myself. But, soon, all that will pass.

MOTHER. (*Sits.*) I pray for it. (VICTOR *crosses to the French doors.*) Enjoy the day.

VICTOR. (*Turns, smiles.*) Remember—trust me. (*She blows him a kiss. He exits.* MOTHER *remains alone On Stage. Slowly, she turns her head to the laboratory, rises and cautiously moves to it. There is a determination in her maneuver. Warily, she tries the door—as if hoping* VICTOR *hadn't locked it after all. She crosses to some bell rope and pulls it. She's nervous, apprehensive.* ELIZABETH *enters Up Center.*)

ELIZABETH. I thought I'd find Victor in here.

MOTHER. He's gone into town with Henry. They had to exchange something.

ELIZABETH. What?

MOTHER. When it comes to Victor's and Henry's experiments, I think it's best not to inquire too closely. Many years ago, I entered that room and was met by a small army of leaping frogs. And there were some peculiar furry things in cages. I've never been back.

ELIZABETH. (*Laughs.*) That does sound like Victor. Even Little William found him unique . . . (*Breaks off.*) I'm sorry . . . I didn't think.

MOTHER. (*Touched.*) I understand, dear. Happens to me all the time. When I'm alone mostly. (*She fights to hold back a tear, uses her handkerchief.* SOPHIE *enters.*) Oh, Sophie, be kind enough to go into the cellar.

SOPHIE. The cellar?

MOTHER. My husband's carpentry table. You'll find an old metal box there. Bring it here.

SOPHIE. Yes, Frau Frankenstein (*She exits.*)

MOTHER. She doesn't like to go down there. She's afraid of spiders.

ELIZABETH. I share her phobia.

MOTHER. (*To business.*) Elizabeth, you know my feelings toward you. When my late husband and I took you into our house, you were a beautiful child. Abandoned, unloved.

ELIZABETH. No, not unloved. You took me to your hearts.

MOTHER. And there is no doubt in my mind that you love Victor.

ELIZABETH. Nor in my mind.

MOTHER. You're good, you're gentle, you're understanding.

ELIZABETH. You make such virtues sound like liabilities.

MOTHER. I don't mean to, only I think there is a great danger in being sisterly.

ELIZABETH. You think Victor looks upon me as a sister?

MOTHER. He will always consider you such unless you give him greater cause to look upon you as a wife. You must be more aggressive with him. Unlike most women you'll have to compete with science. With a man like Victor science can be a formidable rival.

ELIZABETH. If my rival is to be science, I fear I'll always come in second best.

MOTHER. You understand him. As I do. But understanding Victor is not enough. Set your mind to your marriage and let nothing stop you. Don't wait for Victor to see his folly. Marry him. That is the only way. Quick, decisive, total victory.

ELIZABETH. (*Laughs.*) You should have been a matchmaker.

MOTHER. That is exactly what I'm trying to be. Your marriage to my son will be my happiest moment. (*Stands.*) Go after him. Run if you have to. If they suggest you're intruding, then intrude. Hurry. They couldn't have gotten far.

ELIZABETH. But Victor will want to be about his business.

MOTHER. (*Pushes her to the French doors.*) Make his business you, Elizabeth. Do as I say.

ELIZABETH. But, I've never forced myself on Victor.

MOTHER. Exactly. Remember, quick, decisive.

ELIZABETH. (*Smiles brightly, turns.*) Total victory!

MOTHER. Bravo! (ELIZABETH *dashes out.* MOTHER *waves after her.* SOPHIE *returns carrying a metal box.*)

SOPHIE. Is this what you wanted?

MOTHER. (*Crosses over, takes box.*) Yes.

SOPHIE. It's awfully dusty.

MOTHER. Close the door into the garden and draw the drapes. (MOTHER *blows off some dust, moves down to desk, sets the box on top.*)

SOPHIE. The delivery men were here again. There's a package in the hallway addressed to your son.

MOTHER. Who is it from?

SOPHIE. Some chemical shop in Zurich. I think it's glass tubing. (*The French door is shut, the drapes pulled.*)

MOTHER. You can go. I'll call if I need you for anything. (SOPHIE *can see* FRAU FRANKENSTEIN *is nervous about something.*)

SOPHIE. Are you all right, Frau Frankenstein?

MOTHER. Yes, yes. Do as I say. Go about your business, and close the hallway door on your way out. (SOPHIE *exits looking back, concerned.* MOTHER *has opened the box and rummages through until she finds a ring of old keys. She holds them up, looking for a particular one. When she has it, she crosses to the laboratory door. She pauses, reflecting on the merit of her action. She tries the key. It doesn't fit. She tries a second key. Same thing.*) Oh, dear. (*The third key works. She pushes open the door and, apprehensive, enters. Stage remains empty.*)

CREATURE'S VOICE. No! No! Go back! Go back! (*A terrible scream from* FRAU FRANKENSTEIN. *And another. She stumbles back into the study, disoriented, horrified, afraid.* CREATURE *looms up in the doorway.* MOTHER *backs away from him, mesmerized.*)

MOTHER. Get away from me. (CREATURE *comes after her, pleading, hoping, begging for understanding.*)

CREATURE. Do not fear me. Do not scream. (MOTHER *backs Up Center, her breathing coming in tiny gasps, her words tortured. She clutches at her heart.*)

MOTHER. Sophie! Let me be, please! *Sophie!!!* (*She drops to the floor in a spasm of pain, crying out.* CREATURE *drops to his knees and takes her in his arms, sees that she's been frightened to death.*)

CREATURE. (*Sorrowful.*) I meant you no harm. (*He closes her opened eyes and sits there holding the dead woman in his arms as if she were a large broken toy.*) No harm. (*Deeply felt.*) Forgive . . . the Creature.

CURTAIN

ACT TWO

SCENE 2

TIME: *Two days later. RAIN.*

AT RISE: ERNST *stands at the closed French doors looking into the dark garden. SOUND of the rain is soft but audible, on and off, during scene. The room is dark and lamps glow.* SOPHIE *enters Up Center.*

SOPHIE. The carriage is turning into the drive.
ERNST. Nasty weather for a funeral.
SOPHIE. Nasty weather for anything.
ERNST. How is it you didn't go to the cemetery, Sophie?

SOPHIE. (*Emotional.*) I couldn't. I've only been to one funeral in my life. A school friend. I've never forgotten it. I couldn't bear the thought of going through that again with anyone. (*Looks around the room.*) I'd rather remember Frau Frankenstein the way she was.

ERNST. I understand. (*Moves to place where* MOTHER *died.*) You found her here?

SOPHIE. Yes. I heard her cry for me and when I came in she was sprawled out on the floor, her hand over her heart and her face the color of ash.

ERNST. I was unaware that she had a weak heart.

SOPHIE. So was everyone else. But that would be like her. She never was a complainer.

ERNST. Spine like whalebone. She held up like a Prussian during that awful business with Little William.

SOPHIE. (*Wipes away a tear.*) In front of people, yes. She cried herself to sleep many nights, though.

ERNST. Still, the attack came on suddenly, didn't it?

SOPHIE. I got the metal box with the keys from the cellar.

ERNST. Keys?

SOPHIE. She wanted them for something. I found them on the floor.

ERNST. And what became of them?

SOPHIE. I don't know. Herr Frankenstein took them, I think.

ERNST. It's been a strange time. Would you believe there are ghouls at work?

SOPHIE. Ghouls? What kind of ghouls?

ERNST. How many kinds are there? Several graves have been broken into recently.

SOPHIE. That's horrible. Stealing jewelry, I suppose.

ERNST. That I could understand. No, the ghouls didn't take any jewelry—at least in one case.

SOPHIE. What did they take?

ERNST. A foot.

SOPHIE. (*Feeling faint.*) Oh . . .

ERNST. I imagine Victor took the death of his mother hard. (*Sees that* SOPHIE *is faint.*) Are you all right?

SOPHIE. I will be, I think.

ERNST. Didn't mean for my story to upset you.

SOPHIE. (*Frowns.*) Herr Frankenstein's barely spoken a word in two days And he works so hard. He and Herr Clerval.

ERNST. Work?

SOPHIE. (*Nods to door.*) The laboratory.

ERNST. And what is their project?

SOPHIE. Oh, I wouldn't know. No one is permitted in there. It's the one room in the chateau that belongs to Herr Frankenstein alone. I don't know how they manage to get all the machinery in.

ERNST. Machinery? What kind of machinery? (*As the dialogue continues,* ERNST *crosses to the laboratory door.*)

SOPHIE. Wires and rods and electrical bulbs. Things like that. I don't know much about such matters.

ERNST. (*Tries door.*) And you say he's secretive about what he's doing?

SOPHIE. Oh, yes. It's his way. When he get involved in his work he's like a machine himself.

ERNST. Still, it can't do his health any good. Odd. This door is locked from the outside.

SOPHIE. He refuses to take care of himself. Eats almost nothing.

ERNST. When I last saw him I had the impression he was on the verge of a collapse. Seemed exhausted.

SOPHIE. That hasn't changed, I'm afraid.

ERNST. (*Moves back to* SOPHIE.) It's been a bitter season for Victor Frankenstein. His brother murdered, his mother taken so suddenly. I was fond of Victor's mother. A fine woman.

SOPHIE. (*Chokes back another tear.*) Yes, sir. (VICTOR *and* ELIZABETH *enter Up Center.* ELIZABETH *wears black with a mourning veil.* VICTOR *has a black armband on.* HENRY *follows them into the room.*)

ELIZABETH. You here, Inspector General?

ERNST. (*Bow and salute.*) Allow me to extend my deepest sympathy to you, Fraulein, and to you, Victor.

VICTOR. Thank you, Ernst. (ELIZABETH *throws back her mourning veil.*)

SOPHIE. Should I make tea?

ELIZABETH. Please do, Sophie. We're all chilled. So dark, so cold out.

SOPHIE. I'll make some biscuits, too.

ELIZABETH. You might take the umbrellas to the kitchen and dry them. (*To* VICTOR.) Your mother never liked to dry them out in the hallway. (SOPHIE *begins to sob.* ELIZABETH *moves to her.*)

SOPHIE. Poor, poor Frau Frankenstein.

ELIZABETH. (*Comfortingly.*) Now, now, Sophie.

SOPHIE. I am sorry. Forgive me. I . . . I can't believe she's gone. I can't.

ELIZABETH. None of us can. Pull yourself together and go along to the kitchen.

SOPHIE. (*Exiting.*) Yes, Fraulein. Tea won't be long.

ELIZABETH. She's taken it hard. Sophie was so devoted. (*Takes out handkerchief, sits on sofa.*) I know what she feels. I can't get used to the idea myself. Doesn't seem possible. So unreal. I can't understand it. Alive and vibrant one moment—gone the next.

HENRY. Sudden heart failure. Not uncommon.

ELIZABETH. I leave the medical reasons to you, Henry. There's no comfort in them for me. I shall always remember her as the dearest, kindest woman I have ever known. (VICTOR *crosses to sofa, takes her hand.*)

VICTOR. I'll need your strength, Elizabeth.

ELIZABETH. (*Forces a brave smile.*) And you shall have it. The memory of your mother sustains me.

VICTOR. This is most kind of you, Ernst, to stop by.

ERNST. Actually, I am here for two reasons.

HENRY. Two?

ERNST. The first you know. My sympathy.

VICTOR. Yes, yes.

ERNST. And the second— (*He breaks off.*)

VICTOR. Well?

ERNST. The girl—

VICTOR. What girl?

ERNST. Justine.

HENRY. You don't mean the gypsy girl?

ERNST. I do.

VICTOR. What about her?

ERNST. Ordinarily, I'd deny her request, but since we're transporting her to prison today and the wagon had to come this way, I thought—

HENRY. (*Infuriated.*) You thought what?

ERNST. She begs to speak with you, Victor. I agreed. Her hanging is scheduled within the week. A last request you might say.

VICTOR. You want me to see her—in here?

HENRY. That's outrageous.

ERNST. You could come to the prison if you prefer. However, it's a forbidding place. I thought this would be more convenient.

HENRY. (*Still annoyed.*) Perhaps Victor does not wish to have the girl in his home. Or to visit her in prison. You come here because of her request on this day of all days?

ERNST. If I've offended, forgive me. I shall, of course, continue the journey with further interruption.

VICTOR. Why does she want to see me?

ERNST. I'm not sure, but she's asked for this meeting many times.

VICTOR. I'll see her.

HENRY. (*Alarmed.*) Victor.

ELIZABETH. Do you think that's wise?

HENRY. I forbid it. I absolutely forbid it.

VICTOR. (*Insistent.*) I will see the girl.

ERNST. She's an interesting case.

HENRY. Your most interesting, I imagine.

ERNST. Not really. There's been a rash of grave robbery lately.

ELIZABETH. (*Upset.*) Oh.

ERNST. I'm afraid I've done it again. I'm not what you'd call a sensitive man.

HENRY. Do you expect an argument on that point?

ERNST. (*Anxious to retreat.*) The wagon is on the side road. I'll bring her myself. (*At the French doors.*) May I go through the garden?

VICTOR. (*Lost in his thoughts.*) What?

ERNST. The garden. Would that be all right?

VICTOR. Certainly. (ERNST *exits.* HENRY *moves towards* VICTOR *and* ELIZABETH.)

HENRY. The Inspector General is a lout.

ELIZABETH. He means well.

HENRY. There is absolutely no excuse to bring her here.

VICTOR. He's only trying to do his duty.

HENRY. Duty!

ELIZABETH. Henry, what's come over you?

HENRY. (*Quiets down.*) I'm upset. Forgive my outburst.

ELIZABETH. Shouting won't help any of us.

HENRY. I don't think it's wise to see this girl.

VICTOR. I *want* to see her.

ELIZABETH. (*Stands.*) I'll ask that you excuse me, Victor.

VICTOR. (*Walks with her to Up Center.*) You'd better lie down. Rest.

ELIZABETH. I'll try. (*Emotionally drained, she exits.*)

HENRY. It's madness for you to see the girl.

VICTOR. Poor thing.

HENRY. She's a bad sort. Ernst said so himself.

VICTOR. I was referring to Elizabeth. I know her so well. When no one is looking she'll cry. Like my mother. That's why she's gone to her room.

HENRY. She's gone to her room to avoid seeing this Justine.

VICTOR. Did you notice Elizabeth at the graveside? Standing straight. Strong. As if she were telling my dear mother that she was here to carry on and to rest easy.

HENRY. First time I've ever heard you wax sentimental.

VICTOR. First time I've ever felt sentimental.

HENRY. You've taken it all remarkably well.

VICTOR. (*Cynical.*) Have I?

HENRY. I admire you for it.

VICTOR. Do you think because I haven't cried that I've felt nothing?

HENRY. I didn't mean to imply that.

VICTOR. My unseen tears are angry feelings. (*Points to lab door.*) Birth, life, death—stitched together without a seam. If that "thing" had never been born, my mother would be with us now.

HENRY. Don't start that again.

VICTOR. Who is responsible? I am, Henry. I am.

HENRY. Whatever could have possessed her to go into the laboratory?

VICTOR. Curiosity, a desire to discover. We, of all people, should understand that. Can she ever forgive me?

HENRY. I'm sure she does.

VICTOR. And the Creature, the monster, the devil—do you know what he thinks of? My pain? No. He thinks only of his bride. He tells me, "The sooner she is ready, the sooner I am out of your life. Work faster and avoid future misfortune."

HENRY. Perhaps we should heed those words.

VICTOR. He has no more feeling for my mother's death than I would have for a dying flea. He is a thing of stone.

HENRY. He's right. The sooner we get to work, the sooner all this is ended.

VICTOR. I wonder at you, Henry. More and more.

From your honest scientific inquiry has come a mirror image of myself. Do you not fear him now?

HENRY. (*Doesn't want to answer.*) I . . . I . . .

VICTOR. You *do* fear him. (ERNST *returns with* JUSTINE. *She's young, pretty, forceful. She wears a colorful Romany or gypsy costume.*)

ERNST. (*Holding her tightly by the arm.*) No trouble or tricks. Say what you have to say and be quick. (JUSTINE *pulls away from* ERNST *and moves to* HENRY.)

JUSTINE. I was afraid you wouldn't see me. You must believe me, Herr Frankenstein. No one else will. That is why I come here. I wanted to speak to your mother, but they tell me she, too, is dead. For that, I am sorry and sorry again.

HENRY. I am not Herr Frankenstein. (*Nods.*) That is he. (*She turns to* VICTOR.)

JUSTINE. No one will believe my story.

VICTOR. And if I did?

JUSTINE. Do not make fun of me, sir.

VICTOR. I do not, I assure you.

JUSTINE. There *was* a man. A terrible man. With great stitches across his face. I screamed when I saw him, and he held out the cross. It was as if he wanted to give me something to stop my screaming.

ERNST. (*Scoffs.*) And, of course, he said nothing.

JUSTINE. No, nothing. Once I had the cross in my hand, he turned and ran into the woods.

ERNST. Naturally, it was your impulse to strike camp, come into the city, and attempt to sell the gold cross.

VICTOR. Let her tell it in her own words, Inspector General. (ERNST *frowns.*)

JUSTINE. I wanted no part of that cross.

HENRY. You could have thrown it away.

ERNST. No profit in that. (*Sees* VICTOR'S *irritation.*) Sorry.

VICTOR. You're certain he said nothing to you?

JUSTINE. I am, sir.

HENRY. He made no attempt to harm you, that's correct, isn't it?

JUSTINE. (*Brightens.*) Then you do believe me?

HENRY. I . . . I . . .

ERNST. Her sort knows how to play on one's emotions, Herr Clerval. Come along, you've had your visit.

VICTOR. Wait. (*Concerned.*) When will you be hanged?

JUSTINE. I have only a few days more of life. There is no hope for me. The insides of jails and prisons are familiar to me, sir. I've known them ever since I can remember. I was born in a prison. My mother died in one.

ERNST. Bad blood.

JUSTINE. (*Flashes anger.*) My blood is as good as yours and better than most.

ERNST. Mind your tongue.

JUSTINE. (*Takes* VICTOR's *hand.*) I have come here, sir, knowing that my life is to be a short one. But wicked as some may think I am, and I won't deny I've done things I'm ashamed of, I have some decency. Before my maker in heaven and before you, Victor Frankenstein, I swear I am *innocent.* Look into my face, into my eyes, into my soul and tell me if what you see is murder? (VICTOR *cups her face in his hands.*)

VICTOR. Into your face . . . into your eyes . . . into your soul . . . what do I see? Yes, I see *Murder!* (Louder.) Murder! (*Louder still.*) *Murder!*

HENRY. (*To* ERNST.) Get her out of here.

JUSTINE. (*Pulling at* VICTOR.) I swear it! It's the truth! I didn't kill anyone! You must believe me! *Someone* must believe me! Have pity! Pity! (ERNST *pulls her toward the French doors.*)

ERNST. What I get for being soft hearted. Come along. Leave these gentlemen to their business.

JUSTINE. (*As* ERNST *drags her off.*) *I am innocent!* (VICTOR *is shaken. He slaps his hands to his ears to block out her cries.* HENRY *crosses to the decanter, pours a glass and returns to* VICTOR *who gulps down the liquid.*)

HENRY. Are you all right?

VICTOR. You still don't see the ugliness of it? The cruel shame? Now that girl will hang because of the Creature.

HENRY. Circumstances.

VICTOR. She cried "pity" asking for life. So did he. His word has come back to haunt me.

HENRY. (*Shift in mood.*) My notes are almost complete. Let's move quickly, without thinking, pushed on by the knowledge some good will come of all this.

VICTOR. You'll let him go? Escape?

HENRY. I trust his word. I have no reason to doubt it.

VICTOR. Knowing him to be destructive and wrathful?

HENRY. Only because man has made him so. Let them go and find whatever Eden will have them.

VICTOR. (*Low, flat.*) No.

HENRY. What?

VICTOR. I said—no.

HENRY. What do you mean?

VICTOR. You haven't lived with him as I have. Sensing his moods, his unspoken questions. Knowing, always knowing, that if he were ever to gain an upper hand, he wouldn't hesitate to use it. (*Door to laboratory opens.* VICTOR *and* HENRY *turn. A second-or-two passes and the* CREATURE *enters.*) Listening at the door again?

CREATURE. Yes.

VICTOR. Did you hear the girl?

CREATURE. I remember her.

VICTOR. Now another will die because of you.

CREATURE. You had only to point to your laboratory and the girl would have gone free. I remained quiet. But so did you.

HENRY. Victor, when we have finished with our task we'll see what can be done about the girl.

VICTOR. What can be done?

HENRY. I don't know, but we'll think of something.

VICTOR. So easy. Simple. "We'll think of something." And if we don't?

HENRY. I suggest we continue our work.

VICTOR. I no longer have the strength. I would advise you to seek happiness in tranquillity, Henry. Avoid ambition.

HENRY. You have no right to say that, Victor. Because you have been blasted in your hopes, is no reason to assume another may not succeed.

VICTOR. I will not continue.

CREATURE. (*Angry.*) I can make you so wretched that the light of day will be hateful to you.

VICTOR. You have already succeeded in that.

CREATURE. You are my creator, but I am your master.

VICTOR. Never.

CREATURE. Return to the laboratory.

VICTOR. No.

CREATURE. Continue the work.

VICTOR. I refuse.

CREATURE. (*Menacingly.*) You will not deny me my bride.

VICTOR. There, Henry. Did you hear it? The tone of those words. Low, threatening, dangerous. Your "victim" can be your victimizer very quickly. Oh, he's sly, and clever, and quick. He can argue and stroke and persuade, but if the winds turn against him how quickly the devil in the monster shines out.

CREATURE. Keep your vow. Create for me a bride. (VICTOR *shakes his head. Negative.*) Shall each man find a wife for his bosom, and each beast have his mate, and I be alone? (*His fury intensifying.*) Are you to be happy while I grovel in despair?

VICTOR. How can I be happy, how can I be content when all the horror of my misguided zeal stands before me threatening and evil?

HENRY. Victor, calm down. (*To* CREATURE.) Both of you.

CREATURE. (*Furious.*) *Silence.* (*To* VICTOR.) You can blast my other passions, but take care. Revenge will remain.

VICTOR. So be it! (*With that,* VICTOR *darts across the room to the laboratory door, opens it, disappears inside, bolting the door behind him.*)

HENRY. (*Runs to the door.*) Victor, Victor!

CREATURE. I will kill you, Frankenstein!

HENRY. (*Pounding at the door.*) Victor, no! No! Victor, Victor! (*SOUND of mechanical apparatus. Flashes of light from laboratory. The* CREATURE *moves to the door.*)

CREATURE. I will kill! (*Quickly,* HENRY *turns, hoping to placate the* CREATURE. *The flashing lights and the NOISE of the machinery grows louder and louder. See production notes.*)

HENRY. Let me talk to him, let me persuade him.

CREATURE. *Kill him!*

HENRY. I beg of you. Listen to me! (HENRY *attempts to push the* CREATURE *back.*) Listen!

CREATURE. *Kill!* (*With that the* CREATURE *shoots out his arms and throttles* HENRY *by the neck.* HENRY *gags, making horrible choking sounds. The* CREATURE *smashes his fist into the back of* HENRY'S *neck and he crumples to the floor in a dying gasp. Suddenly there is a terrific ROAR from behind the laboratory door and the STAGE LIGHTING FLASHES UP AND DOWN WILDLY. The* CREATURE *looks all around bewildered, stunned, realizing that the sound and lights indicate that his bride is forever doomed. The* CREATURE *lifts his arms to the insane flickers of LIGHT as the NOISE continues to grow in volume. His cry is painful, awful in its pathetic appeal.*) Wife . . . companion . . . friend . . . No-o-o-o-o-o . . . (*His cry fades like an echo. The* CREATURE *buries his face in his hands and drops to his knees. The LIGHTING RETURNS TO*

NORMAL. A few seconds pass and we realize the CREATURE *is sobbing. Laboratory door opens and* VICTOR *steps out.*)

VICTOR. Finished . . . ended. (*Slowly, the* CREATURE *lowers his hands. There is a look of almost unbelievable hatred and rage on his face.*)

CREATURE. For this, you will pay even more.

VICTOR. Do not poison the air with your malice.

CREATURE. (*Low, growling.*) You will pay.

VICTOR. Leave me. (CREATURE *stands, moves to French doors. Sees the prostrate form of* HENRY.) Henry . . . (*Crosses to the body, kneels beside it. He turns* HENRY *over in his arms, reacts.*) Dead . . . Henry, too . . . dead . . .

CREATURE. I go, Frankenstein, but remember—*I shall be with you on your wedding night.* (*SOUND of rain increases. The* CREATURE *steps into the windswept garden.*)

CURTAIN

ACT TWO

SCENE 3

AT RISE: *SOUND of wind. Scene begins as a continuation of the play's opening with* VICTOR *and* ELIZABETH, *in her wedding gown, seated on the sofa.* VICTOR *is finishing his strange story.*

VICTOR. (*Recalling* CREATURE'S *prophesy.*) ". . . I shall be with you on your wedding night." (*Repeats.*) "On your wedding night." (ELIZABETH *stands, moves Center.*)

ELIZABETH. If only you had confided in me earlier.

VICTOR. I was afraid.

ELIZABETH. Of what I would think?

VICTOR. And of what you would say. A thousand other fears, too. Most of all—that you would judge me mad.

ELIZABETH. What torture it must have been for you.

VICTOR. You can never know.

ELIZABETH. Poor darling.

VICTOR. Don't waste sympathy on me. If I had been content to search for the philosopher's stone, or the elixir of life, our wedding wouldn't be like this.

ELIZABETH. He hates you so much that he would kill you on this night of all nights?

VICTOR. What better night to destroy his maker? I denied him his bride and, now, he will deny me my life.

ELIZABETH. It will never come to pass.

VICTOR. I wish I could believe that.

ELIZABETH. You must. I believe it and so must you.

VICTOR. Oh, Elizabeth, I am truly blessed. If only this horrid vision of his return could be wiped away.

ELIZABETH. Do you recall "The Ancient Mariner"?

VICTOR. Coleridge? We read it one summer.

ELIZABETH. Yes. (*Recites.*)
>   "Like one who, on a lonely road,
>   Doth walk in fear and dread,
>   And, having once turned round, walks on,
>   And turns no more his head."

VICTOR.
>   "Because he knows a frightful fiend
>   Doth close behind him tread."

(*He stands, takes* ELIZABETH *in his arms.*) Ernst has the chateau surrounded.

ELIZABETH. Then you're safe.

VICTOR. Perhaps.

ELIZABETH. They'll see him if he comes close to the house.

VICTOR. I hope so.

ELIZABETH. Victor, you must always trust me. Never keep anything from me.

VICTOR. If I live through this night.

ELIZABETH. (*Covers his mouth with her hand.*) Never, never say that again.

VICTOR. Do you realize that if he does kill me, the Creature will have succeeded in destroying the House of Frankenstein? (ERNST *has entered through the garden in time to overhear this remark.*)

ERNST. I assure you, Victor, the Creature will not elude my net. I have a dozen men staked around the chateau. With shotguns that would bring down a charging rhinoceros.

VICTOR. You do not know him as I do. He's brilliant in his strategies.

ERNST. I flatter myself that I, too, have considerable skills in that direction.

ELIZABETH. There is no danger, then?

ERNST. The minute the Creature is sighted an alarm will go up. After that, it is merely a matter of seconds before I bring the beast to his knees.

ELIZABETH. Perhaps he won't show up.

ERNST. We've considered that. For his sake it would be better if he didn't. From my point of view I would not wish it. It will give me considerable pleasure to either destroy him, or chain him to the wall of a madhouse or an asylum for the criminally insane.

VICTOR. And the gypsy girl?

ERNST. We haven't released her yet. No telling what stories she'd carry. No need to unduly alarm the citizenry.

VICTOR. But she will go free?

ERNST. All in good time. (SOPHIE *enters Up Center.*)

ELIZABETH. You see, Victor, you have nothing to fear.

ERNST. Stay in the house. Don't venture outside under any circumstances. I must insist on that.

VICTOR. You have our word. (ERNST *exits Up Center.*)

SOPHIE. Can I get you anything, Frau Frankenstein?

ELIZABETH. "Frau" Frankenstein. How odd that sounds. My married name. (*Lighter mood.*) No, Sophie, thank you. Nothing. Oh, draw the drapes. It's so chilly in here.

SOPHIE. Would you like a fire?

ELIZABETH. No. The drapes will be fine. (SOPHIE *sets about the business of pulling shut the drapes Up Center. When this is done she draws the drapes at the French doors, closing them, too. Dialogue continues through this business.*)

VICTOR. I was thinking something quite terrible. Yet, it may have ended for the better.

ELIZABETH. You're thinking of Henry.

VICTOR. Yes. I don't think anything but death would have stopped his quest. I infected him as surely as if I had injected him with a strange and forbidden venom. Once he tasted what I had savored his doom was sealed. Odd that I have survived and he has not.

ELIZABETH. I shan't listen to any more of this. (*Strong, resolute.*) We will get through the night. And tomorrow we will make plans for travel. Greece would be lovely this time of the year. Maybe Italy.

VICTOR. There are a few things I must do.

ELIZABETH. When?

VICTOR. Now. In the laboratory.

ELIZABETH. (*Stunned.*) You can't be serious.

VICTOR. I have many things to destroy. The machinery, the lighting panels, the generator. (*Crosses to his desk and picks up ledgers, papers, etc. When* SOPHIE *is through, she waits by the French doors.*) And these. Most of all *these.* The ledgers, the notebooks.

ELIZABETH. Must you do it now?

VICTOR. You needn't be afraid. Come with me to the laboratory.

ELIZABETH. (*Recoils.*) No . . . I never want to go in there. I think I shall seal the room forever. Wall it up or tear it out.

VICTOR. Sophie.

SOPHIE. Yes, sir.

VICTOR. Go into the garden and ask one of the men to stay here with my wife.

SOPHIE. You want me to go out there?

ELIZABETH. I'll be quite all right.

VICTOR. Sophie, do as I ask.

SOPHIE. Yes, sir. (*Terrified, she turns and exits through the drapes at the French doors and into the garden.*)

VICTOR. (*Crosses for the laboratory, ledgers, etc., in his arms.*) When these go up in flame I will have made some amends for my sins.

ELIZABETH. Then it should be a private act. Do it quickly, Victor. Hurry back to me. (*VICTOR looks at her lovingly, exits into the laboratory. ELIZABETH is left Onstage. Suddenly, it dawns on her that being alone on such a night has slight compensation. She looks about nervously. SOUND of wind whips up. The curtains at the French doors rustle.*)

ELIZABETH. Sophie? (*She turns. Nothing. She talks to herself.*) Must get hold of myself. There is nothing to fear. Nothing. (*From the laboratory comes the SOUND of the machinery, as if VICTOR were, once again, up to something questionable. ELIZABETH reacts.*) Victor? (*She crosses to the laboratory door and rattles it. It's locked.*) Victor? (*Now comes the unmistakeable SOUND of someone moving behind the drapes Up Center. The drapes rustle. ELIZABETH sees the movement.*) Who's there? (*Nothing. As the SOUND of the machinery hums from behind the door, the lighting in the shadowy room DIMS UP and then DOWN, UP AND DOWN.*) Who's there? Who is it? Ernst? (*Mesmerized, ELIZABETH moves toward the drapes Up Center. SOUND of the laboratory business continues. ELIZABETH walks like a somnambulist. Closer and closer to the drapes. Her breathing is heavy, audible. Her hand reaches for the drapery and just as she's about to pull the sections apart*—SOPHIE *darts in via the French doors.*)

SOPHIE. (*Fast.*) Frau Frankenstein. (*Startled,* ELIZABETH *gives a startled half-muted scream.*)

ELIZABETH. Sophie . . .

SOPHIE. The policeman will be here in a moment. I'll go and show him the way. (*With that,* SOPHIE *turns and hurries out.* ELIZABETH *is still frightened, barely able to get out her words.*)

ELIZABETH. Sophie . . . no, wait . . . Sophie . . . (ELIZABETH *turns, moves for the laboratory, set on getting* VICTOR *to open the door.*) Victor, Victor! (*Up Center draperies are flung apart revealing the* CREATURE. *With his wild hateful stare, and his arms spread wide he is a horrifying figure, made all the more so by the DIMMING UP AND DOWN of the room's lighting and the constant hum of the laboratory apparatus.* ELIZABETH *turns, sees him in one fast movement, screams.*)

CREATURE. There is a better way to make Victor Frankenstein suffer. (*Points.*) You, you the bride of my maker, shall die in his place!

ELIZABETH. Victor, Victor! (ELIZABETH *runs for the laboratory door. The machinery and the lights are still performing. She bangs on the door.*) Victor, he's here! He's here. (*The* CREATURE *advances and* ELIZABETH *moves into the center of the room.*)

CREATURE. I have never left this house. I have lived under the eaves of the attic . . . waiting . . . waiting. I shall be with you on your wedding night.

ELIZABETH. Please . . . spare us.

CREATURE. Even your cries for mercy give me pleasure, for I think of the words of my bride that I shall never hear. You must die and Frankenstein must suffer! (*He reaches out and grabs her by the throat, his back to the laboratory door.*)

ELIZABETH. (*Struggling.*) No, no—Victor, *Victor!!!*

CREATURE. Die, die, die! (*Suddenly, the door to the*

laboratory flings open and VICTOR *enters with a revolver. He FIRES. Once . . . twice . . . three times. Each time the hot lead supposedly tears into the* CREATURE *he recoils as if taking the impact. He lets go of* ELIZABETH *who, choking, her hand at her throat, struggles to the Upstage chair. The* CREATURE *makes his way to the drapes at the French doors, clutching his side. He turns once to look at* VICTOR *and holds one hand out as if pleading. Sorrowfully.*) Frankenstein . . . (VICTOR *fires again. The* CREATURE *bares his teeth viciously, stumbles into the garden.* VICTOR *moves quickly to* ELIZABETH.)

VICTOR. It was *you* he was going to destroy. He would let me live knowing what my life would be like. (*Close to her.*) Elizabeth, forgive me. (*By now, the STAGE LIGHTING is BACK TO NORMAL.*)

ELIZABETH. (*Gasping for breath.*) I'm . . . all right . . . all right . . . (VICTOR *quickly moves to the decanter and pours her a glass.*)

VICTOR. His mind is as keen and bright and crafty as ever. I should have guessed what he planned.

ELIZABETH. It's over . . . (VICTOR *moves to her with the glass.*)

VICTOR. Here, drink this. (*From Offstage Left we hear the distant SOUNDS of gunfire.* VICTOR *and* ELIZABETH *exchange a worried look. The brandy.*) Finish it. (ELIZABETH *empties the glass.*) More? (*She shakes her head no.* SOPHIE *runs in through the French doors.*)

SOPHIE. They are after him!

VICTOR. Did you see him?

SOPHIE. Only as he ran past the police. Who was he? No one will tell me a thing.

VICTOR. Which path did he take?

SOPHIE. He ran toward the water. The lake.

VICTOR. Get some smelling salts.

SOPHIE. I don't need them.

VICTOR. (*Irritated.*) Not for you. For my wife.

SOPHIE. Yes, sir. Right away. (SOPHIE *exits Up Center.* ELIZABETH *takes* VICTOR'S *hand.*)

VICTOR. Why didn't you call out?

ELIZABETH. I did. Over and over. But the laboratory door was bolted and there was so much noise from the machinery.

VICTOR. You'll never hear that sound in 'his house again. I have destroyed my records, the apparatus, all that remains is the memory. (ERNST *enters via the French doors.* ELIZABETH *and* VICTOR *stand together, close.*) Well?

ERNST. He ran into the lake.

VICTOR. He's dead?

ERNST. Nothing could have survived my fusillade.

VICTOR. But did you see him fall, or go beneath the water?

ERNST. He was stumbling, mortally wounded. My men will drag the lake for his body. You may rest easy, Victor. Elizabeth. The Creature is no more. If you'll excuse me, I'll return ɔ my men. (*He salutes, bows professionally in the military manner, exits.* VICTOR *moves to the French doors, pulls aside the drapes, peers out.* ELIZABETH *moves Up Center.*)

VICTOR. The work of my hands is finished. I have destroyed what I have created. Full circle.

ELIZABETH. Come along.

VICTOR. I could almost feel compassion for him.

ELIZABETH. I do feel it.

VICTOR. You, too?

ELIZABETH. It's ended, Victor. Forever.

VICTOR. (*Still looking toward the lake. Thoughtfully—*) I wonder. (*He turns, sees* ELIZABETH *smiling gently. He smiles in return, moves toward her. They exit Up Center.*)

CURTAIN

END OF PLAY

PRODUCTION NOTES

ON STAGE:
Drapes at Up Center, drapes at French doors, books and book-
shelves, sofa, 2 fine chairs, desk and chair, papers, ledgers
(desk), anatomy chart, paperweight, tape measure, pen, framed
photograph of William, lamp, writing paper, decanter and
glasses, magnifying glass, bell rope. Additional stage dressing
as desired: paintings, rugs, small tables, vases, lamps, etc.

ACT ONE

BROUGHT ON:
Revolver, bullets, gold cross (Ernst), book (Henry), bridal
bouquet (Elizabeth), keys (Victor), breakfast tray with bowl
of strawberries (Sophie), hat box with wedding veil (Elizabeth)

ACT TWO

Bundle with hand (Henry), metal box with keys (Sophie),
black mourning veil (Elizabeth), black arm band (Victor),
handkerchief (Elizabeth), revolver (Victor)

SOUND EFFECTS:
Machinery, rain, wind, gunfire.

COSTUMES:
The wardrobing of the play follows the usual 1880's–1900
fashions. The following are listed specifically only because of
some required dramatic effect.

ACT ONE

Police uniform and hat (Ernst), bridal gown (Elizabeth),
nightgown and robe (Mother), doctor's white smock (Victor),
dark, threadbare garb (Creature)

ACT TWO

Surgical smock, mask, cap (Victor), smock (Henry), gypsy
costume (Justine)

SUGGESTIONS

Remember, the more "atmospheric" the set the more impact the play will have. If the Up Center entrance and French doors could be elevated somewhat, it would make the comings and goings more effective. Beware of lighting the study too brightly except when called for. Also, make certain that the SOUND of the machinery is audible enough for the audience to hear clearly. This need holds true when Victor fires his revolver at The Creature during the play's conclusion. Since Victor fires from just outside the laboratory door, the shots can be fired from Off-Down Stage Right, if desired. But they must be LOUD. Jarring the audience and provoking a little nervous laughter won't hurt. *Nothing is more damaging* to a scene where gunfire is required than to have the sound of the shots weak and obviously phony. A good effect can be achieved by having The Creature conceal a plastic bag filled with stage blood and when the shots are fired, he can tear at the bag with a razor blade and hold out a bloodied hand to Victor. Also, remember that the drape business in the last scene, with the Creature hiding, should be built up for terror and audience suspense. Don't rush it. Caution the actor portraying Victor to remove the black arm band between the second and third scene of the second act. Papier-mache or painted tennis balls work nicely when the Creature tests the strength of his grip.

ABOUT THE "CREATURE"

The Creature of Mary Shelley is not the monster of the film versions. He was tall, yes, but beyond that normal in most physical respects.

The true horror lies in the fact that he is "artificially created" from bits and pieces of dead men.

This point is hammered in the play, as well as the fact he is "stitched together." Keeping this in mind, his makeup should reveal many stitches. Corners of the mouth, neck, eyes, forehead, as well as at the wrist. Perhaps a bolt or two here and there. Again, it's important that the audience be able to see the artificial aspects. Some clumsy boots help to enhance the effect and his costume should be dark and threadbare and homespun in appearance. The jacket should be too short in the sleeves to give a "gangling" effect.

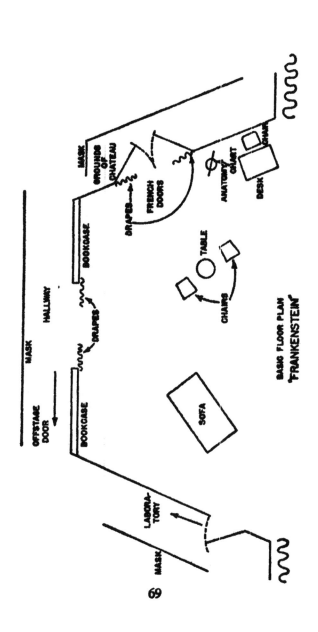

BASIC FLOOR PLAN
"FRANKENSTEIN"

MASK

OFFSTAGE
DOOR

BOOKCASE

DRAPES

HALLWAY

DRAPES

BOOKCASE

MASK

GROUNDS
OF
CHATEAU

DRAPES

FRENCH
DOORS

ANATOMY
CHART

DESK

CHAIR

TABLE

CHAIRS

SOFA

LABORA-
TORY

MASK

69

TREASURE ISLAND
Ken Ludwig

All Groups / Adventure / 10m, 1f (doubling) / Areas
Based on the masterful adventure novel by Robert Louis Stevenson, *Treasure Island* is a stunning yarn of piracy on the tropical seas. It begins at an inn on the Devon coast of England in 1775 and quickly becomes an unforgettable tale of treachery and mayhem featuring a host of legendary swashbucklers including the dangerous Billy Bones (played unforgettably in the movies by Lionel Barrymore), the sinister two-timing Israel Hands, the brassy woman pirate Anne Bonney, and the hideous form of evil incarnate, Blind Pew. At the center of it all are Jim Hawkins, a 14-year-old boy who longs for adventure, and the infamous Long John Silver, who is a complex study of good and evil, perhaps the most famous hero-villain of all time. Silver is an unscrupulous buccaneer-rogue whose greedy quest for gold, coupled with his affection for Jim, cannot help but win the heart of every soul who has ever longed for romance, treasure and adventure.

WHITE BUFFALO
Don Zolidis

Drama / 3m, 2f (plus chorus)/ Unit Set

Based on actual events, WHITE BUFFALO tells the story of the miracle birth of a white buffalo calf on a small farm in southern Wisconsin. When Carol Gelling discovers that one of the buffalo on her farm is born white in color, she thinks nothing more of it than a curiosity. Soon, however, she learns that this is the fulfillment of an ancient prophecy believed by the Sioux to bring peace on earth and unity to all mankind. Her little farm is quickly overwhelmed with religious pilgrims, bringing her into contact with a culture and faith that is wholly unfamiliar to her. When a mysterious businessman offers to buy the calf for two million dollars, Carol is thrown into doubt about whether to profit from the religious beliefs of others or to keep true to a spirituality she knows nothing about.

Lightning Source UK Ltd.
Milton Keynes UK
UKHW021044030120
356275UK00006B/157/P

9 780573 609176